Dear Reader,

Home, family, community and love. These are the values we cherish most in our lives—the ideals that ground us, comfort us, move us. They certainly provide the perfect inspiration around which to build a romance collection that will touch the heart.

And so we are thrilled to have the opportunity to introduce you to the Harlequin Heartwarming collection. Each of these special stories is a wholesome, heartfelt romance imbued with the traditional values so important to you. They are books you can share proudly with friends and family. And the authors featured in this collection are some of the most talented storytellers writing today, including favorites such as Brenda Novak, Janice Kay Johnson, Jillian Hart and Patricia Davids. We've selected these stories especially for you based on their overriding qualities of emotion and tenderness, and they center around your favorite themes—children, weddings, second chances, the reunion of families, the quest to find a true home and, of course, sweet romance.

So curl up in your favorite chair, relax and prepare for a heartwarming reading experience!

Sincerely,

The Editors

MAE NUNN

grew up in Houston and graduated from the
University of Texas with a degree in communications.
When she fell for a transplanted Englishman living in
Atlanta, she moved to Georgia and made an effort to
behave like a Southern belle. But when she found that
her husband was quite agreeable to life as a born-
again Texan, Mae happily returned to her cowgirl
roots and cowboy boots! In 2008 Mae retired from
thirty years of corporate life to focus on her career
as a full-time author.

HARLEQUIN HEARTWARMING

Mae Nunn

More Room for Love

TORONTO NEW YORK LONDON
AMSTERDAM PARIS SYDNEY HAMBURG
STOCKHOLM ATHENS TOKYO MILAN MADRID
PRAGUE WARSAW BUDAPEST AUCKLAND

Recycling programs
for this product may
not exist in your area.

ISBN-13: 978-0-373-36563-0

MORE ROOM FOR LOVE

Copyright © 2012 by Mae Nunn

Originally published as MOM IN THE MIDDLE
Copyright © 2007 by Mae Nunn

More Room for Love

This book is for my darlin' Michael.

I couldn't make it through a single day without your boundless love and infectious laughter. You are my rock, my champion, my best friend, my personal chef and my very own cowboy. I adore you!

CHAPTER ONE

"MAMA!" ABBY CRAMER screamed.

Her mother had suddenly collapsed, one leg folded awkwardly beneath her thin body. Abby kept a hand on the shopping cart that held her toddler and dropped to her knees on the concrete floor of the new home-improvement center.

"What happened?" The young cashier bolted around her checkout counter and knelt beside Abby.

Her mother clenched her teeth against the obvious pain. "My foot slipped out from under me." She twisted at the waist in an effort to get up, then fell back with a gasp. The character lines in her pale face deepened with the grimace.

Abby knew her very private parent would die of pain before she'd suffer the embarrassment of tears in public.

"Don't worry about your little boy. I'm

right here beside him." A woman's voice penetrated Abby's concern. She nodded thanks, let go of the cart and turned full attention to her mother, who once again strained to sit up.

"Please lay still. You might have broken something." Abby began the assessment she'd learned during first-aid training. The skills had served her well in her three years as an elementary schoolteacher. Her mother's hands fluttered like the wings of an angry bird, shooing away Abby's efforts to feel for injuries.

"Oh, I've just aggravated my old sciatic back. I'll be okay in a few minutes." She held her breath through a determined effort to ease her twisted leg from its abnormal position. Finally giving up, she rested her head on the floor.

The store employee untied her apron, rolled the cloth into a pillow and maneuvered it beneath short-clipped, salt-and-pepper hair.

"Don't move. I'll get Guy," the cashier insisted as her sneakers squeaked a fast departure toward the back of the new store.

Concerned onlookers stopped to offer assistance. Abby reached for her mother's hand, only to be brushed away.

Being the late-in-life only child of Sarah Reagan was both a blessing and a curse. Responsibility and kindness were civic requirements of the woman who was more like a finishing school headmistress than a doting parent. While Abby's mother expected her daughter to help others, Sarah generally refused aid at all cost.

Abby's gaze darted from the scene on the slick concrete floor to her precious toddler son who perched in the shopping cart above her. Dillon's chubby legs dangled as he leaned forward and frowned over the excitement below. She smiled to reassure him, mouthed a silent *Thank you* to the thoughtful female who hovered nearby.

"Where's my purse, Abigail?"

"It's still on the counter."

"Well, hand it to me before somebody steals my wallet."

Abby reached for the pastel spring bag and offered the other shoppers an apologetic shrug before placing the straw purse within her mother's reach.

"I don't want to worry your father about this so let's not mention it when we get to the house."

"Mama, we're going to have to go to the hospital to make sure you don't have a serious injury."

"Nonsense," Sarah insisted. But the word was hardly out when she yelped involuntarily, arching her back from the stab of pain.

"I have to agree with your daughter." A man squatted beside Abby, his orange apron announcing the grand opening of yet another new Hearth and Home Super Center. "We've put in a call to a private ambulance service. They'll be here any minute to take you to Brackenridge."

"No, thank you," Sarah insisted. "A senior citizen on a fixed income can't afford a luxury like that. Besides, a hospital will just run expensive tests, take my money, and tell me I'm fine." Sarah's hands felt for the buttons of her seersucker jacket, making sure she was properly covered. "As soon as I catch my breath, Abigail can take me home."

Handsome blue eyes, glinting with unspoken conspiracy sought Abby's permission to take charge of the situation. She nodded slightly, glad to have somebody else deal with her hardheaded parent if only for a few moments.

"I'm afraid that's not possible, ma'am. It's Hearth and Home's standard operating procedure for any injury, no matter how minor, to be treated as an emergency. You wouldn't want me to lose my job for not following store policy, would you?" He turned his palms upward in a plea for cooperation.

Abby watched with fascination as her perpetually demanding mother became agreeable and compliant beneath the mesmerizing appeal of those blue eyes. The hard lines of her face softened as she sighed her acquiescence.

"And don't worry about the cost. Hearth and Home will cover everything."

"I don't expect any charity," she insisted.

"Well, maybe this time you'll make an exception and let the store's insurance take care of things."

He patted her thin hand, *and she didn't jerk away.*

Torn between relief and envy, Abby filed

that moment away for consideration on another day.

A gust of warm wind whipped her curls as the glass doors slid apart. In the distance she heard the sounds of a gurney's legs snapping into place and then the rush of rubber wheels and crepe soles that brought the paramedics to their side.

"Pardon us, folks. Please step aside, miss," the efficient attendant instructed as he took charge. "We'll take it from here." He knelt to assess the situation.

"At least you had the good sense not to scare me half to death with your siren," her mother half complimented, half grumbled to the EMT.

"You can thank Mr. Hardy for that."

"Guy Hardy at your service, ma'am." The man with eyes the color of Texas bluebonnets nodded. "I figured you were in enough discomfort without that racket ringing in your ears."

Her mother seemed focused on Guy's smiling face and charming words. She hardly noticed the work of the crew who deftly lifted her from the hard floor to the padded gurney for the short trip to the boxy red ambulance.

Abby noted the sudden flash of uncertainty in her mother's eyes at the same moment Dillon began to whimper. Accustomed to adjusting on the fly to meet the needs of her classroom full of first graders, Abby considered her dilemma; her mother on the way to the hospital and her son on the way to panic. To make matters worse, her dad was home alone, sitting in front of the television in his wheelchair, waiting for his "womenfolk" to return with his list of plumbing supplies.

Though it was a mild spring day, Abby's cheeks filled with unaccustomed heat. She hadn't let the death of her husband send her into a downward spiral and she wouldn't let this crisis put her into a tailspin either.

"We'll take my vehicle." Guy Hardy had whipped the orange apron from around his waist and handed it to the cashier. "I'll drive you and…" He was glancing toward Abby's blubbering son.

"Dillon. My son's name is Dillon."

"I'll drive you and Dillon to Brackenridge

and stay with you until they release your mother."

"But what about our van?" she asked, though she'd already scooped up the baby and her shoulder bag and followed quickly behind this take-charge man.

"You're too distracted to be driving right now anyway."

GUY GUIDED THE LOVELY young woman and her son to a white H&H courtesy SUV parked outside.

"I need to get Dillon's car seat."

"No problem. Climb in and tell me where you're parked."

Focused as he was on the task at hand, he couldn't help admiring the shiny cap of blond curls that bobbed across his field of vision as she stepped up into his vehicle, clutching the baby boy who bawled over his unfamiliar surroundings. Her confident handling of the toddler reminded Guy of his sisters and the same second-nature manner they showed with their kids.

He followed her directions and pulled alongside a minivan coated with a layer of yellow pollen, a common sign of springtime in Austin, Texas. She dropped the keys into his outstretched hand, allowed him to retrieve the car seat and help her carefully secure it and the boy together with her in the backseat.

"I'll have you there in no time."

"Thanks," was all she said. She dug into the oversize bag probably filled with all the traditional goodies mommies kept handy to appease grumpy babies. She hardly spoke a word during the fifteen-minute trip, but cooed softly to her son while he gnawed what looked like a hunk of graham cracker.

Guy allowed her the privacy she needed to comfort her child and steel herself for whatever waited at the hospital. He drove carefully, checking his passengers often in his rearview mirror. During one glance he noticed that her face was turned to the side, offering a clear view of her profile. Thick lashes framed eyes crinkled with worry. The perfectly straight bridge of her nose suited her firm jaw. Both probably genetic signs of stubbornness, from her mother's side of the family.

She shoved a hand through her hair tucking

curls behind one ear. Her head was covered with the same kind of ringlets that he'd teased Casey about for years. He still remembered the wallop his youngest sister had delivered to his gut the day he'd called her Corkscrew one too many times. At the memory he felt an uncontrollable grin of brotherly love.

"Wanna share the joke? I could use some humor right now."

He glanced over his right shoulder briefly, training his smile her way. What she returned was a watered-down imitation. The effort stirred sympathy in his heart.

"Your hair reminds me of my kid sister, and I was just remembering how I used to make fun of it."

Her eyes widened, brows rose in an exaggerated manner as she attempted to look offended. "So you think I have funny-looking hair, huh?" She shook her curls at her son, who burst into high-pitched giggles. "Well, you're not the only one."

"My sister's curls are wild and corky, she's always trying to squash them into submission. But yours are…" Their eyes met in the mirror. Hers filled with anticipation of what he might say. "Nice."

She stared for a couple of seconds then smiled and ducked her head as if no one had complimented her for a long time.

Unbidden, protective warmth surged in his chest for this young woman. Her quiet modesty reminded him of Kate, one of his older sisters, the busy mother of four boys and an incredible wife in the mold of their beloved mother.

With so many great examples of married couples in his family, it was odd—even to him—that he truly had no need whatsoever to experience that for himself. Not that there was any chance of it with his work schedule. As vice president of corporate expansion, he was on a tight schedule to open an H&H Super Center in a new city every twelve months. He'd be buried with projects through the end of the decade.

"Thank you. A girl will take *nice* over *wild and corky,* any day."

"Actually, Casey's hair is part of the reason she's the prettiest of my sisters, though I'd *never* admit that to her," he said as he took the final turn that would lead them to downtown Austin's premier emergency-care facility.

"How many sisters do you have?"

"Five," he said into the rearview mirror.

"What are their names?" Abby's wide eyes were back.

"I won't bore you with the long versions. But they go by Meg, Kate, Andrea, Tess and Casey. I came along between Andrea and Tess."

"What was it like growing up in a house with that many women?" She seemed amused at the thought. The tiny glimmer of humor in her eyes was charming.

"Brutal." He chuckled. "They spoiled me rotten. Between Mom and the girls, every need was met before I could ask a second time. By grade school I'd figured out that the kid-glove approach with my sisters would always get me what I wanted."

"Well, I hope Dillon has a sister to be soft on some day. But not *five*," she teased and again his heart surged with compassion. This young woman had so much on her mind yet she was putting him at ease.

"Here we are," he warned as he pulled into the hospital's emergency entrance.

The ambulance attendants had already wheeled their patient through the automatic doors and disappeared into the triage unit. Guy hurried around to help his passenger step down.

"I'll be right in as soon as I park."

With an efficiency that amazed him, Abby slung the heavy-looking bag over her shoulder and propped the boy on her hip. She offered a grateful smile and hurried into the building.

Forty-five minutes later there was still no news. Guy checked the time on his watch against the display on his cell phone. Two o'clock. He returned it to the clip-on holster and shifted in the waiting-room chair that was far too low and narrow for the comfort of a man of his stature. Once again he reminded himself that he had to do something about the extra ten pounds that years of eating on the run had added to his six-foot-one frame. But his mother was constantly telling him he looked better with a little more meat on his bones. He stretched his long legs and crossed one ankle over the other to admire his newest pair of custom-made cowboy boots, constantly impressed with the craftsmanship of Texas boot-makers. The kangaroo leather of the handmade Luccheses had molded nicely to his size-twelve feet during the four months he'd worn them. Soon they'd be stretched by cedar shoe trees and lined up with a dozen other pairs made of everything from ostrich to boa constrictor. It would be a pity to retire these boots but that was his way of marking the end of a project, acknowledging it was successful.

Though he'd consumed his weight in antacids, a new H&H was open and running relatively smoothly.

Until today.

Well, he'd remain hopeful and positive, put this minor crisis behind him and be moving on to the next site in no time. In a couple weeks Casey would arrive to take the handoff. He'd head home to Iowa where he'd jump knee-deep into new construction planning for the Galveston location. Austin had been nice but he was eagerly looking forward to fishing the waters of the bay during his tour of duty in Galveston.

A fussy-baby wail interrupted his personal musings. He glanced up and spotted Abby heading his way with little Dillon clinging to her for dear life. Guy jumped to his feet and took several steps in her direction.

"Any news?"

"Still waiting on a doctor to read the X-rays." She jostled the boy and shushed him, having no apparent impact at all as his complaints grew louder. She pressed his face to her shoulder in a useless effort to muffle the sobs.

"I'm sorry, it's way past his nap time and he's had all the cookies he's going to get until he eats some vegetables."

"Can I give it a try?" Guy raised his arms, hands open, ready to take Dillon. With ten nieces and nephews, he was handy with a cranky toddler if he did say so himself.

"I don't think so." The skepticism on her face almost made Guy want to laugh. "He won't let you hold him. My dad's the only man Dillon's used to."

"Your husband's not good with little ones, huh?"

"I'm a widow," she said softly.

His jaw clenched along with his insides as he realized his verbal gaffe and the complicated facts that accompanied her simple response. She was a young woman alone, so much weight on her slender shoulders and without the love and support of a husband, that treasure the married women in his family prized above all else.

"I'm so sorry. I didn't mean to make things worse for you."

"Don't feel badly. It's been nearly two years and it's a common assumption when you have a toddler, so I'm almost used to it."

The boy whined louder.

"I really am pretty good with a grumpy baby," he assured her, remembering his sister Tess's wedding day when he'd been officially appointed to make sure none of the little ones got out of sorts during the reception. Good thing it was his policy never to take a date to a family function, because these days the girls expected Uncle Guy to be their babysitter.

Dillon strained against his mother's efforts to rest his head on her shoulder and his blubbering continued with gusto. His face was contorted in aggravation when he turned his head toward Guy.

"Hey, little pal," Guy used his best cajoling tone and nodded toward the nearby glass wall that overlooked the hospital's courtyard. "Wanna go look out the window?" He held his palms out, but not too close.

Briefly distracted from his misery, Dillon's crying stopped. He snuffled and hiccupped while his mother smoothed the face that was remarkably free of tears. He peered at Guy, who used the positive sign to take a small step closer and smile. The boy looked to his mother for guidance.

"Go see birdies?" she encouraged. "Tweet, tweet, tweet."

His head bobbed and he leaned away from his mama, reaching chubby arms outward. Guy scooped up the boy, amazed by how heavy the little tyke felt.

"Whoa, this fella is solid."

"Tell me about it." Her eyes were round. She was clearly surprised that Dillon had left the security of her arms. She shrugged, then dropped her large purse on a nearby chair and rotated her shoulders. The latest revelation as well as the creases across her forehead told Guy the contents of the bag were nothing compared to the weight on this woman who was not much more than a girl herself.

"Mrs. Cramer? Dr. Cabot is ready to speak with you now," a nurse called.

Abby turned toward the voice, then back to Guy and her son. Worry deepened the lines in her pretty face. She leaned to retrieve the bag and Guy knew Dillon would naturally be next.

"Go ahead. Leave him with me. We'll be fine and you can give the doctor your undivided attention."

She squinted, seemed unsure what to do.

"Weet, weet!" Dillon squealed and pointed toward the window.

"You betcha." Guy smiled and repositioned the boy to face the wide pane of glass and the oversize birdbath outside that held his attention. "He's happy, so we'll wait right here." He tipped his head toward the waiting nurse. "Go."

Abby let the bag fall back on the floor and turned away. Her low heels tapped a rapid beat against the linoleum floor as she hurried to learn the condition of her mother. After she disappeared through the gray swinging doors, Guy carried Dillon for a closer look at the pair of daredevil mockingbirds at play.

Twenty minutes later she was back. Her fair skin had lost its appealing color. She pinched her bottom lip between her teeth and wrapped her arms across her torso, as if holding in what strength she had left. Dillon's head had slumped to Guy's shoulder, heavy with the need for a nap. Guy folded himself into a nearby chair and motioned for Abby to join him. She collapsed on the next seat and accepted her sleeping boy.

"Her hip's broken," her voice quavered. "It's called a spontaneous fracture." She dipped her face to kiss Dillon's head, blocking Guy's view of her private emotions.

"Oh, no." He spoke softly, understanding the implications. He knew from the experience with his paternal grandfather that the injury could be a long painful recovery, a permanent disability or even worse if complications set in. The outcome for her family could be dire.

"And they'd moved her around so much it

was obvious she was suffering. That was hard to watch." Her voice was a whisper.

If she'd been one of his sisters, Guy would have wrapped Abby in his arms and rocked her along with the sleeping toddler. But she was a customer whose mother had just suffered a major injury on his family's property. He didn't dare touch her for fear of further complicating an already difficult situation that could potentially impact the lives of his family, the H&H shareholders and their employees.

He sat straighter in his chair, pushed aside his own concerns. His worries were insignificant compared to Abby's.

"Did they give her pain meds?"

She glanced up, nodded. "Something really strong so she'd rest. But she was rattling off instructions for me and the nurses when she fell asleep." A sad smile flickered across her face and Guy mirrored her expression, imagining his mother doing the same, ordering the hospital staff about if the situation were reversed.

"Will she need surgery?"

"Dr. Cabot doesn't think so. He says she'll

be in the hospital for a few days and if everything goes well she'll be released to a rehab facility for extended physical therapy. As usual, she's more worried about Daddy than she is about herself." Abby sighed and rested her head against the back of the chair. "In forty-eight years of marriage my parents have never spent more than a few days apart. I don't know how I'm going to keep them both occupied for six weeks with everything else I've got to do, but I'll manage somehow."

"Abigail?" A heavyset woman in a floral-print housedress hurried toward them.

"Oh, thank you for coming, Mrs. Eller." Abby rocked forward and used momentum to swing Dillon onto her shoulder as she stood. Guy hopped to his feet as he was introduced to Abby's neighbor. The two women exchanged a quick hug over the sleeping boy.

"What room is your mama in? I'll sit with her so you can go tell your daddy."

"You didn't say anything to him, did you?" Abby sounded worried.

"Oh, no. Now you hurry on home before he gets suspicious about what's taking so long."

Guy lifted Abby's blue fabric bag sprinkled with dozens of fuzzy yellow chicks and slung it across his shoulder then followed her through the hospital's emergency exit.

"Would you like me to take you straight home?"

"I appreciate the offer, but I'll need my van to bring Daddy back to the hospital."

"I can give you both a ride," Guy offered as he held open the door of the Hearth and Home SUV.

She shook her head, blond curls bobbing. "Dad's in a wheelchair and the side door of the van is outfitted with a lift."

Guy grimaced at the new information. *Another* hardship for this small family. How would Abby cope with the situation? You never knew the true measure of someone until their back was against the wall and their only choices were to crumble or come out fighting.

No matter the circumstances of the injury, the corporation bore certain liability for accidents on their property. In this case it would be Guy's responsibility to do everything possible to avoid litigation. The fact that the potential threat came in such a charming form would have nothing to do with his desire to help a woman out of a crisis.

Or would it?

He glanced at Abby Cramer. The sheen in her brown eyes said she needed more than assurances that medical expenses would be covered. Staying close to this situation would allow him to do two things—watch out for his family's business interests and give Abby someone to lean on.

She squared her shoulders in a proud profile that suggested she'd carried her burden alone for a long time.

Would she be as stubborn as her mother or would Abby Cramer let him help her?

CHAPTER TWO

ON MONDAY AFTERNOON, Guy stood on the porch steps of the Reagans' modest brick home.

"I'm coming! Hold your horses," a male voice called from behind the front door.

Guy shifted the box of bulky plumbing supplies to his left arm and stuffed his right hand into the front pocket of his store apron to deposit his keys. He glanced toward the driveway where he'd parked the Hearth and Home truck. He'd planned to bring the purchase by the previous day but his phone calls had gone unanswered. Since he'd concluded Abby and her father must be spending all their time at the hospital, he was surprised to get a response when he'd punched the doorbell three times in quick succession.

The door creaked open an inch but no face appeared. Guy squinted to see inside the dark house.

"Down here, drugstore cowboy," the aggravated voice grumbled an obvious reference to the fancy boots.

Guy glanced down, his gaze locking with dark eyes beneath an overhang of bushy gray brows.

Abby's father.

Guy estimated the man to be in his late seventies, but the long, thin body sunken into the inexpensive low-slung wheelchair could have made him look older than his years. Guy extended his hand.

"Guy Hardy, sir. Hearth and Home Super Center."

"Pete Reagan. Friends call me Shorty, mostly because I'm not." His eyes raked Guy up and down. "Guess you can, too."

The old fellow kept the handshake brief.

Needing an excuse to be standing on the man's porch, Guy nodded toward the box he carried. "I brought the supplies your wife and daughter left at the store on Saturday. Thought you might need them."

"Women." Shorty shook his head. "You can't live with 'em, can't trade 'em for catfish bait." A rusty hinge complained as he pushed the door wider and maneuvered his chair to the left. After moving a few feet he stopped, leaned to one side and pulled a thin wallet from his hip pocket.

"How much?"

Guy watched as bony hands counted out several bills.

"That's covered, sir. I'm just making the delivery."

The bushy brows drew together. "Then how much for the delivery?"

"There's no charge, Mr. Reagan."

Shorty folded together a couple of one-dollar bills and thrust out the offering. "Then take this for your trouble. I insist."

Guy suppressed a smile as he accepted the modest tip. "Why, thank you, sir. May I carry this inside for you? The parts shift pretty easily so this box might be hard to manage."

"Well, since you've decided I'm an invalid, and you've already got my money, you might as well haul them all the way back to the laundry room yourself."

Guy winced. He hadn't meant for the comment to come across as an insult, especially since he was normally so conscientious. Life with a houseful of women had taught him to choose his words carefully. That was even more important with customers.

"I need to be mindful of my words," he muttered.

"Say what?" Shorty snapped.

"Nothing, sir."

"Well, stop talkin' to yourself and come on." He spun the chair, offering a good look at the back of his mostly bald head fringed with wisps of silver.

"And for pity's sake try to keep up, Roy Rogers," he grumbled over his shoulder as he set his chair in motion.

Thinking Abby's sweet disposition deserved high marks after growing up with a stern mother and grouchy dad, Guy hefted the carton and stepped across the threshold. He hurried to follow the man who was quickly disappearing down the long hallway. When Shorty stopped abruptly at the door of what appeared to be a utility room, Guy slipped inside the small, musty-smelling space. A washer-and-dryer pair were positioned to the left, and to his right a deep utility sink was installed in the countertop. Open cabinet doors beneath the sink exposed a bucket that caught the puddle created by a dripping faucet.

"Just sit it down there," Shorty gestured toward the floor. "Maybe Abby and I can get around to it tomorrow after we visit Sarah."

"If you don't mind me asking, sir, how is Mrs. Reagan?"

"Doc put a pin in her hip yesterday morning."

"Oh, I thought that wasn't going to be necessary."

"It was a last-minute decision," he explained. "Surgeon says it'll get her back on her feet sooner."

"Is she in much pain?"

"She's holding up. Won't complain. Never does. But it's driving her crazy that she's not here to tell me what to do." A trace of a smile glimmered for the first time. His gray eyes lit with mischief and Guy caught the resemblance between Dillon and his grandpa. Hadn't Abby said her parents had rarely been separated in forty-some-odd years of marriage? The old guy was probably missing his wife like crazy. No wonder he was out of sorts.

Guy deposited the box filled with brass pipes and silicon gaskets for replacing the trap and waste elbow of a sink, and then glanced toward the plumbing repair efforts.

"Okay if I take a look?" Guy asked permission.

"Knock yourself out."

He squatted to get a better view of the work in progress. Actually, not much work had been done at all. Beyond dismantling the old pipes and stuffing a bucket under the open drain, nothing more had been accomplished.

"You do much plumbing, sir?"

"Back in the day. My legs are mostly useless now so it's impossible to get up and down like I once did. My baby girl helps me."

"Abby?" Guy couldn't quite envision the head covered with soft golden curls studying the workings of a rusted drain.

"Don't sound so surprised. She's pretty handy with a wrench as long as her old man is giving the instructions."

As intriguing as the image of Abby Cramer wielding a tool was, Guy realized home repairs were just one more area where she probably had to take charge for her parents.

"I have a little experience with plumbing. How about if I finish this up for you?"

Shorty opened his mouth to speak, most likely to object. But then he snapped it shut and glanced at the clock on the laundry-room wall.

"Won't your boss be expecting you back at the store?"

"No, sir. The company encourages employees to assist customers anytime we can, and I happen to be free for the rest of the afternoon."

Shorty squinted, seemed reluctant to accept the offer.

"You gonna charge me by the hour?"

"There wouldn't be any cost involved, sir, as long as you don't mind helping me out with some pointers," Guy added. "It's been a while since I tackled anything this complicated."

"Complicated? Ha!" The old man snorted. "This is so easy a Girl Scout could handle it." He scooted his chair close to the carton of parts, leaned forward and began poking through the hardware.

Guy felt a smile curve his lips as he enjoyed the sight of Shorty Reagan checking the inventory of the box against the list scrawled on a white index card.

"Well, don't just stand there grinnin' like some cowpoke on payday while those fancy boots of yours gouge Sarah's linoleum," Shorty snapped. "Grab that adjustable pipe wrench and let's get to work."

AS ABBY PULLED TO a stop against the curb in front of her family home, she glanced toward the Hearth and Home truck that blocked her driveway. She wrestled Dillon from his car seat, both of their stomachs grumbling the loud need for dinner. She'd make grilled-cheese sandwiches for herself and her dad while Dillon mauled a bowl of beanie weenie, and then they'd all load back up and head for another evening at the hospital. It had only been a couple of days and already she was drained from the long hours of work and worry. Her parents' life together had been a continuous string of crises and they were taking this latest one in stride.

But Abby knew how hard it was on them to be apart. Their love for one another had gotten them through three miscarriages, her father's battle with multiple sclerosis, financial disaster, the tragic loss of their son-in-law, and now this. Six weeks of in-patient rehab stretched in front of them, then who knew how long before they could return to a normal life.

Not that life would ever be *normal* again without Phillip, the best friend of her childhood, her husband for less than a year and the father of a son he would never know.

With Dillon on her hip, Abby trudged up the porch steps and jostled her key against the dead bolt. The door opened easily, not locked, not even closed securely. She frowned, knowing her mother would not approve of such carelessness.

"Dad?" she called.

Instead of the usual squeaking of rubber wheels on the oak planks, she was greeted by the rumble of masculine voices from the end of the hall. Actually, it wasn't a greeting at all. Her father hadn't even acknowledged her. If not for the conversational sound of the men, she'd fear something was terribly wrong.

"Daddy?" she called for him again as she walked the dark hallway.

His wheelchair sat in the laundry room doorway.

Empty.

She gasped and tightened her arm around Dillon, who yelped his discontent.

"In here, baby girl."

Then she spotted him. Seated cross-legged on the floor was her seventy-six-year-old father. Beside him stretched a pair of legs in blue jeans, with an orange H&H apron draped over the waistband. The man wore a white polo shirt stretched tight across his abdomen. She could see very little of his arms and nothing of his head since the top quarter of his body was crammed beneath her mother's utility sink.

But there was no mistaking the identity of the Hearth and Home employee. The fancy cowboy boots gave Guy Hardy away.

"Daddy, what are you doing on the floor?"

"Giving this man a badly needed lesson in drain replacement."

"Hi, Abby," Guy's muffled voice greeted her from inside the cabinet. "Was that Dillon I heard?"

"Weet, weet!" Dillon responded to his name and kicked his feet to be released.

"Hey, Guy," she returned the greeting. The first relief she'd felt for days surged through her heart at the sight of her father enjoying himself over a simple plumbing repair. The perfect distraction. "I see you've met the other man in my life."

"And this one is every bit as charming as Dillon," Guy answered.

Her dad grunted and glowered up at her from his spot on the floor.

"Weet, weet!" Dillon squirmed, wanting to join the men.

"Hey, little buddy," Guy acknowledged her son, who obviously recognized the voice.

"We're just about finished here," her father said. Despite the deep creases around his eyes, she sensed his skeptical approval for their company. "Give us fifteen minutes and then I'll get cleaned up to go see your mother."

"You go ahead, sir. A couple more turns of this wrench and we're done."

Her dad nodded and began the difficult task of climbing back into his chair. Abby choked down the desire to offer help as he struggled to hoist himself up into the seat. He was determined to be independent despite the primary progressive stage of the disease that he'd lived with for as long as she could recall. The inflammation in his spinal cord had made walking impossible for several years but he insisted on being self-sufficient in every other way.

Respect for her father's wishes and worry for his weakened upper body churned her emotions. Fearing the chair would topple from his efforts, she decided to help whether he wanted it or not. She squatted and released Dillon. He chuckled with delight, no doubt over escaping his mama's grasp, and toddled toward his papa.

"Here, let me give you a hand with that, sir."

She looked up to see Guy, already on his feet, offering the assistance she was positive her father would reject. Guy had braced the wheels against the cabinet and was gently supporting her father so he could settle comfortably into the leather seat of his chair.

"Thanks." Her dad huffed out a breath,

sounding relieved. "Getting down is always a sight easier than the climb back up. I coulda made it by myself, though. Always do." Abby heard the gruffness and wondered if Guy had any idea it was there to mask the gratitude so hard for her father to show.

The two men exchanged respectful nods. Dillon stood at their side, watching, holding his arms outward, literally drooling to be in the middle of the awkward maleness.

"Papa! Weet, weet!"

The moment pulsed with something that distinctly excluded her.

A sort of *male bonding*. Her insides twisted into a tight knot.

That was exactly what seemed to be going on, and something about this emotional picture was all wrong. Phillip should have been the man helping her father, ruffling the hair on Dillon's head, hoisting him up into his papa's lap for a ride into the kitchen.

But Phillip had left her. Voluntarily. Now he was gone. Permanently.

How could life be so cruel?

"I know your family has things to do and I apologize that I'm still underfoot." Guy watched her dad and Dillon cruise the hallway and then turned to her. "I'll just clean up here and be on my way."

"Thank you," she softly spoke the words, knowing he deserved them, determined to deny the constant stabs of resentment that had taken hold of her heart at the news of Phillip's death.

"It's kind of you to spend time with my dad. He's a tad irascible with Mama in the hospital, and your visit seems to have distracted him for a bit. Once again, you're a lifesaver."

He held up his palms deflecting the praise. "Hey, I'm just a regular guy trying to walk the walk the company teaches. When I saw he needed help, I offered to stick around. Any H&H employee would do the same." He downplayed his kindness.

She let her shoulders slump, relaxing for the first time all day. It was nice to meet a simple man who believed in acts of kindness.

"I'll mop up back here later," she gestured to the spatters of grimy water on the utility-room floor. "But right now we have to grab a sandwich and get to the hospital before visiting hours are over."

"Hey, no problem. I'll just pick up this mess, put away the tools and show myself to the door." He squatted and began loading rusted pipes into the cardboard box. "By the way, your dad's really something."

"Yeah, I agree." She nodded and turned to leave the utility room.

"And quite the talker," he added with a note of amusement in his voice.

Afraid to ask what that meant, she kept moving.

True to his word, Guy Hardy finished up the work, and ten minutes later poked his head into the kitchen to say goodbye. He declined the offer of a sandwich and even insisted on letting himself out as if he'd done it a hundred times.

Abby rose to put her plate in the sink and glanced toward the family room. Through the large picture window she could see the driveway was once again empty. He was probably halfway back to the store that would be open for several more hours.

"Dad, if you'll wash Dillon's face, I'll go

freshen up and we'll still have time to stop at the market for that bunch of flowers you wanted to get Mama."

As Abby passed the laundry-room door, she glanced inside, expecting to find wet traces of their sink repair. Instead, the white linoleum floor was much cleaner than usual. The mop was thoughtfully replaced, damp end upward, in the hanging utility rack. This regular guy, as he called himself, was nice *and* a clean freak.

She sighed, knowing there was only one way to handle this. With the bedroom door closed, she asked directory assistance for the new Hearth and Home Super Center. After the cheery greeting, Abby requested the store manager. Following a brief hold, a woman's voice answered.

"I'm Leah Miller, and it's my pleasure to serve you."

"This is Abby Cramer and I left some things there on Saturday after my mother's accident."

"Oh, yes, Mrs. Cramer," the voice was filled with concern. "If there's any way we can be of help to your family, you just let us know."

"Well, thank you for the kind offer, but I was really calling for another reason. I'd like to compliment one of your employees. He delivered everything today and then stuck around to help my father with a plumbing repair."

"That's the kind of story we like to hear about our personnel. Can you give me the employee's name, please?"

"He's the same person who took us to the hospital. His name is Guy. Guy Hardy. Do you think you could put a note in his file so it will look good on his work record?"

"Ma'am, I don't think I'll be able to do that," the woman sounded amused. "Guy doesn't have an employee file. Not in Austin, anyway."

"I don't understand." Abby squinted at herself in the mirror above her dresser.

"Guy's the boss," Leah said simply.

"But I thought you were the manager."

"Yes, ma'am, that's true. I'm the manager, but Guy Hardy is the owner."

Abby watched her own reaction in the mirror as her jaw sagged with the realization.

There was nothing at all regular about this Guy.

CHAPTER THREE

ABBY FASTENED HER seat belt and slammed the door of the van.

Well, that explains it. The nice-guy act had nothing to do with genuine kindness and everything to do with protecting his interests. When will I learn not to be such a Pollyanna?

She shifted into Reverse, turned to glance behind her and looked at her precious boy. He'd dozed off the moment he'd settled into his car seat. Her father was silent for once, busy with his own thoughts. The quiet was a welcome relief from all the chatter of her first graders. The school year was winding down. Coming to a screeching halt, actually. She was preparing her kids for the testing that would assess not only their skills but her ability as a teacher. With the burgeoning Hispanic population in Texas, many children required special attention because English was their second language. She could teach twelve

hours a day and not meet everybody's needs.
The playground project was behind schedule, underfunded and she still hadn't found
a weekend sitter so she could devote more
time to its completion. School would be out
just after Mother's Day, the day of the playground unveiling, and there was more on her
to-do list than she could possibly accomplish
in what little free time she had.

And now it looked like she might have
a battle with an insurance company on her
hands. The true identity of Guy "Good Sa-
maritan" Hardy was just one more brick in
the wall that was weighing heavily on Abby's heart. On Saturday he'd insisted the store
would cover her mother's medical expenses,
but that was when he'd thought Hearth and
Home might somehow be responsible. Now
that they had the diagnosis of a spontaneous
fracture, would the store try to weasel out?
Would their insurance provider be like the
others, washing their hands of the case and
leaving her folks to fill in the gap that would
surely be left once Medicare benefits were
paid? They'd had enough setbacks during her
father's battle with MS to know how quickly

the bills could pile up. Abby hoped they wouldn't have to rely on assistance. Again.

The hospital parking lot was full and once more she was grateful for the handicapped spaces up front.

"Daddy, you go on in and stay as long as you'd like," she offered as they entered the building. "I'll sit out here with Dillon."

"You sure were quiet on the way here, baby girl. I know you've got a lot on your plate right now, but you don't need to worry about me and your mama. We'll be fine."

Her daddy wheeled the manual chair that should have been replaced ages ago out of sight and Abby sank down onto a waiting-room sofa.

"If life continues on this course," she muttered to herself, "we're in a heap of trouble."

THE NEXT AFTERNOON, Guy climbed down Shorty's stepladder and flipped the switch by the kitchen door. The ceiling fan overhead whirred to life, sending a gentle rustle of cool air through the room. Guy folded the aluminum ladder, leaned it carefully against the wall, and gave the shiny silver chain that dangled from the new light fixture a tug. The bulbs glowed inside their tulip-cup houses, spreading much-needed illumination across the kitchen countertops.

One last touch and the job would be finished. He fished in the pocket of his Hearth and Home apron, drew out a small, faceted glass prism, and clipped it to the end of the pull chain. He stepped back to admire his work. Perfect.

"Thanks." It was a grumbled gratitude, but sincere nonetheless. "Sarah's been after me and Abby for a year to hang that thing. Now she can enjoy this nice breeze in the kitchen all summer." The grouchy old man who'd met Guy at the door yesterday was still front and center but he'd softened a bit. It was clear it would take a lot of effort to win his approval.

But from Shorty's observations, it would take even more to earn Abby's. To quote Shorty, his daughter was "madder than a wet hen." Twenty-four hours earlier she'd learned Guy's identity from the store manager instead of from him directly. When he'd mentioned the situation to his sister on their nightly call, she'd burst into snorts of laughter.

He could just imagine Casey wiping the tears of mirth from her eyes as she administered a dose of sibling wisdom.

"I adore you, big bro, but in some areas you're pretty dense, which is why Dad's going to give me your job one day." Her chuckle carried over the phone line. "Just because your five sisters think you hung the moon, it doesn't naturally follow that every woman will love you like we do."

He shook off the memory of the wisecrack. He didn't expect *every woman* to love him, but something about Abby Cramer made him want to be liked, at least a little bit.

The front door creaked open, a signal that she was home much earlier than the day before. Guy made a mental note to oil the hinge, and then quickly changed his mind. Until she'd forgiven his failure to disclose, he probably needed a warning sign that she was in the house.

"Hey, Daddy," she called.

"In the kitchen, baby girl."

Guy lifted the stepladder, carried it through the entry leading to the darkened garage and pulled the door closed behind him. He'd noted earlier that the fluorescent ceiling bulbs were burned out, the overhead door opener was broken and the ventilation was insufficient for the cans of paint stacked on the ancient cinder-block shelves.

"What's he doing here again today, Dad?"

Abby's voice carried through the hollow-core door. Guy grimaced at the question that sounded more like an accusation.

"He came back to help me hang the ceiling fan." Guy smiled as Shorty defended his presence.

"Looks to me like he did more than help. You let him take over another one of our projects."

"That's not quite true. I gave all the instructions and handed him the parts and he managed the rest without too much difficulty. He has apprentice potential, but not much."

"Well, nothing's wrong with the apprentice you already have, Daddy. *Me*."

Guy heard the possessiveness in Abby's voice, recognized it as the same tone Casey took with their father when she was vying with her older siblings for a share of his attention. Guy's natural reaction when Casey got that way was to tell her to suck it up and wait her turn. Somehow he didn't think that was the correct approach with Abby, an only child who'd probably never had to compete for her father's time.

He heard the rumbling of Shorty's lowered voice and stepped closer to the door. Eavesdropping. Casey would call him a jerk and pinch him till he yelped.

"Honey, you have zero time for all the repairs and improvements this house needs and I thought it would be nice if your mama came home to find some of those things finished. I wouldn't admit it to him just yet, but he seems like a nice enough fella. If he wants to help an old man out, what's wrong with that?"

"Don't you see what he's up to, Daddy? That horse's behind is just doing all this to stay on our good side so we won't sue his store over Mama's accident."

"So what if he is. He'll find out soon enough that we're not that kind of people. Besides, as much as I love Dillon, it's nice to have some conversation with a guy who's not wearing a drool bib. Now, come hug your old man and tell me what you're doing home so early."

Guy stamped hard on the wooden step and rattled the loose knob to announce his approach. The brown eyes that greeted him were...different. Her mother's eyes. Stern. Abby had actually called him a *horse's behind!* Worse yet, she seemed determined to remain angry with him, something he'd rarely experienced, and couldn't accept.

"How do you like the fan?" He used the cajoling tone that never failed to work with his sisters.

She turned her face toward the slowly rotating blades, giving him a moment to appreciate her clear skin, the natural blush of her cheeks that were round, like her son's.

Abby studied the new fixture. Except for the twinkling piece of stained glass dangling from the end of the chain, it looked just like the picture on the box.

"Not bad," she muttered. Not exactly praise for a job well done but it was the best she intended to give under the circumstances. Abby knew she'd never be able to speak her mind with her father sitting there like this inter-loper's begrudging champion.

"Dad, would you mind getting me a change of clothes for Dillon?" She needed to get him out of the room. "That little pair of denim overalls and a clean T-shirt would be nice."

"Where is he? Is anything wrong?"

"Everything's fine," she assured her father. "The day care called and he got fruit punch down the front of his shirt today. I thought I'd pick you up first then we'd change Dillon at the day care and go to the hospital before dinner."

"Sure. That'll be a nice surprise for Sarah."

"Speaking of nice surprises," she turned to Guy. "That certainly was a breathtaking arrangement the store sent yesterday, and I noticed you personally signed the card. Of course, you hardly know our family, or you'd understand we're simple folks. The five-dol-lar bouquet we took her made my mother just as happy."

"Abby's right. My bride has always appre-ciated small pleasures. A good thing since that's about all we've been able to afford most of our lives. So she was tickled pink by that big crystal vase of flowers." Her father held out his hand. "Will I see you tomorrow?"

Guy accepted the grip. "Absolutely. We need to get started on that list if you want everything shipshape before Mrs. Reagan comes home."

"I'll just get Dillon's things together, then."

When her daddy was out of earshot, Abby turned to Guy, no longer putting on a happy face.

"You can drop the helpful hardware man act. I'm on to you."

"Meaning?" He leveled wide, innocent eyes on her that she bet worked like a charm with the adoring females in his life.

"Meaning, I know you're not just an H&H employee, *you're the owner.* And you're not just worried about my family, you're covering for your own."

"Guilty as charged on all counts." He nodded.

The speech she'd practiced on the drive home flew out the window on the breeze from the new fan.

"That's right. My family owns the stores and it's my job to protect our investment."

"So you admit all this *help* you've been offering is just an act."

"No way."

"Then why didn't you tell me who you were when we first met?"

"I didn't really think it was important to give you my résumé when your mother was lying on the floor of my store."

Ouch, he had her there.

"Besides my parents have raised us to keep our personal business private, so it's not like I have OWNER on the license plate of my company car. The employees know who I am, it's not necessary for every customer to know, too."

She still had reason for her righteous indignation. Didn't she?

"But your customers should know your promise to take care of my mother's medical needs was just PR. She believed you when you said everything would be covered by Hearth and Home or she'd never have agreed to that expensive private ambulance service."

"Abby." He lowered his chin; his shoulders slumped. "I'm sorry I've given you the impression that I'm a dishonest person, but I assure you I didn't lie about the medical coverage. You don't need to worry about the bills. I give you my word on that." He held his hand out as he'd done with her father a couple of minutes earlier.

She felt like a day-old balloon with a pinprick, as all the air seeped out of her argument that he was up to no good. She accepted his hand. A man's grip, warm and solid and strong. A very different touch than she'd ever felt holding hands with Phillip.

"I apologize," she said simply, lost for the proper words after impugning his integrity.

"Apology accepted." He let her off the hook but held on to her hand. "And please accept mine for not introducing myself properly. Dad's taught us to keep a low profile with customers, but it was never my intention to hide my identity."

"I see." She nodded and eased her hand out of his warm grip. "Now what's all this about a list?" She changed the subject.

He fished an index card covered in her father's handwriting from his back pocket.

"Shorty and I wrote up a list of all the repairs you two have been planning to make. I really need to get out of the new store manager's way and let her run things on her own, so I have some time on my hands before I have to turn over the quality phase of the project to my kid sister, Casey. Believe it or not I really enjoy your dad's company. He reminds me a lot of one of my uncles and I'd like to help take care of these repairs, if you don't disapprove."

Abby glanced at the list, all things she had good intentions of doing one day. Her heart sank just a bit at the thought of missing out on spending this time with her father. The MS was so unpredictable. He could be able one day and bedridden the next. She'd already found out what it was to forever lose precious time with a man she'd loved. She didn't want to waste a single day of the allotment she had left with her father.

"These are all things my daddy and I wanted to do together." She pouted, knowing she probably sounded like a brat.

"Even better. If you have any free time to join us, just grab a hammer and help out."

Now that things were going his way again,

his engaging blue eyes sparkled with mischief, and Abby began to understand why the women in his family had spoiled this guy rotten.

CHAPTER FOUR

"So, I CAN HAVE everything wrapped up and be in Austin next week. It's almost time to start the handoff, you know." Casey's voice buzzed across the phone line reminding Guy of their time line.

Not that he needed reminding.

He looked at the calendar above his desk. As usual, the Warden, as the Hardy clan called Casey, was in control and ahead of schedule. She *couldn't* let a deadline slip. Ooooh noooo. How was it possible that the baby sister he loved more than life could leave him warmhearted and clenched-fisted at the same time? She'd been breathing down his neck since they were kids, competing with him at every turn, determined to best him at his own game.

His parents had never had to challenge their only son. That was Casey's personal mission.

He'd joined the swim team and she'd taken up high diving. He'd gotten voted most likely to succeed; she'd been elected class president. He'd gotten some assistance at the local community college; she'd earned a full scholarship to the University of Iowa. The board had offered him an executive position after seven years; she'd won her title after five.

But he had the plum, the job she'd wanted. When the board had voted on expansion, Guy's business degrees and years of experience had made him their first choice. Casey had taken it remarkably well, then had promptly set a course to study world-class quality processes. He knew it was just a matter of time before she proposed a new security structure that would shake up the way they did business. Not that there was anything wrong with that, but it would be as much to nip at Guy's heels and impress their father as it was to improve corporate work processes.

His youngest sister thrived on competition. Guy had sympathy for any man who fell for her quick wit and easy smile. The combination masked the sharpshooter nature and workaholic tendency that would undoubtedly intimidate the poor guy who found himself in love with Rebecca Thelma Casey Hardy one day.

He picked up his cup of ice, rattled a cube into his mouth and chewed with gusto.

"Alexander Theodore Guy Hardy, stop crunching ice in my ear. Are you even listening to me?"

"You've given me this lecture so many times I can recite it in my sleep. Gimme a second here, I'm looking at my schedule."

Scanning the calendar, he grabbed an orange marker off his desk and drew a dotted line through the next four weeks and circled Mother's Day. At best Sarah Reagan would be out of rehab by that time. He and Shorty had crossed a small project off their list every few days. Now it was time to tackle the big stuff that would make the decades-old, drab little home more accessible for Shorty's old wheelchair and the walker Sarah would undoubtedly need for a while.

"Thanks for being ready to move things up but I don't need you that soon," he muttered into the handset cradled between his ear and shoulder. "In fact, I'm thinking of pushing my departure date out a bit."

Casey was silent. A bad sign. Guy hurried on.

"I'm enjoying the weather here. I might take a few days off and do some fishing."

"Where?" She snorted, an unflattering sound that had always annoyed their mother. "Since when does any game fish besides a trout or a red appeal to a saltwater snob like you? Aren't you all hot to get to Galveston to try out the new waders I gave you for your birthday?"

"Hey, there's some decent-size largemouth in Lake Travis. Thought I'd spend a week checking out the local honey holes."

"Then I should come on down early to keep an eye on things while you're away."

"Casey, give it a rest." He knew she wouldn't be placated easily. Well, he wasn't prepared to give her all the details, just enough to make her back off. "I need to hang around until the woman who broke her hip in the store is out of the rehab hospital and back on her feet. It just wouldn't be right for me to leave before this situation is settled."

"It figures." He could hear the disapproval in her voice. "You've found another cause. Dr. Guy has a new patient to save." While his other sisters praised his willingness to give his time to help people in need, Casey saw it as a weakness. A veil over the voids in his own life. Sometimes he thought she might be onto something. But mostly he realized it was just one more of her tactics to goad him into a challenge.

"This cause is probably in her seventies and she found me, remember?" he reminded Casey, knowing she already had the details noted and memorized.

"Meanwhile I'm just supposed to cool my heels, I suppose?"

"Why don't you call the gaggle and scare up a shopping trip?" He referred to the term their mother used for her five daughters. "I'm sure there must be yet *another* navy-blue Brooks Brothers suit out there reserved for you, Warden. But why don't you try a departure from the Iowa Department of Corrections uniform for a change?"

"Very funny, but it so happens I've lost a

few pounds and could use some new clothes. Maybe I will see what the girls are up to."

"That's the spirit. Part with some of that obscene salary the company is paying you."

"Mind your own business." It was the same answer she gave him every time he suggested that she enjoy life a bit and put some of the small fortune she was earning to good use. Heaven forbid she should do anything fun or philanthropic.

"It was just a suggestion, corkscrew," he poked her sore spot.

"That's it. This conversation has come to an end."

He smiled, mission accomplished. "Talk to you tomorrow night. I love you, Thelma."

"Love you too, Theodore."

Guy dropped the phone in the cradle, folded his hands behind his head and propped his feet against the edge of an open desk drawer in the Heart and Home security office. He pushed the toes of his boots and rocked back in his leather chair to stare at the ceiling.

What he'd said was accurate. Mostly. He couldn't leave town until Sarah and Shorty's situation had improved. They were nice folks who needed a break and Guy had a responsibility to lend a helping hand.

But there was more. He wanted to do the same for their daughter, the real person in need from what he could tell. So far that had been next to impossible. He'd seen very little of Abby the past two weeks. Judging by what Shorty said, she put in a lot of hours between her teaching position and the volunteer work she did. What little free time she had was devoted to her son and parents. Guy did what he could to help by staying out from under her feet and cleaning up after their repair efforts. This weekend that might be difficult since he and Shorty planned to get started on the new deck and wheelchair ramp.

Guy suspected Abby would likely be around the house. Surely she'd be taking a little downtime. He dropped his boots to the floor, rolled the chair back and pushed to his feet. Just in case, he'd make a few peace offerings to leave around the house.

THERE WAS NO DENYING IT. Abby wasn't cutting the mustard in some area of life. What other reason could there be for all the troubles that had heaped upon her for the past two years?

Uncharacteristically grumpy on a sunny weekend morning, she stooped to pull a pair of jeans from the dryer. She smoothed and folded them atop the laundry-room counter, then placed them neatly on the stack.

"Oh, cut the pity party, Abigail," Abby mimicked her mother's stern voice as she reached into the warm appliance and drew out another item.

A nylon jersey had turned inside out during the wash. She flipped the maroon shirt so its right side was visible and hugged it to her body. She buried her face in the soft fading fabric, and swallowed down the sadness that threatened.

Phillip's high-school football jersey. She wore it on nights when sleep was elusive. She closed her eyes, inhaled deeply and recognized a stirring of the anger she would forever feel at his decision to sign up for active duty. It still stung all these months later. How could he put himself in harm's way in the name of duty to his country when she'd needed him so? When she'd been carrying their first child?

She pressed her face into the jersey and inhaled again. Her shoulders sagged with disappointment. Just like Phillip, his scent on the shirt was gone forever.

She should put it in a trunk and save it for Dillon along with the team photos of Phillip, the big number *30* on his chest. Some day Dillon would want to hear all about his daddy and Abby would be ready to tell her son everything about the shy young man who'd been her best friend for as long as she could remember.

She brushed the silky cloth against her cheek and exhaled a sigh. It was still too soon to lock her reminders of Phillip away in a box. She couldn't do it. Not yet.

The thwack of wood striking wood resounded through the laundry-room window that led to the backyard. Abby laid the shirt gently on the counter and swept the curtain back, revealing the scene outside. A white pickup with an H&H sign on the door was backed into the yard, tailgate down. A load of lumber jutted from the bed.

Guy slid the planks out two at a time and tossed them into a pile by the driveway. The orange T-shirt was tight across his broad shoulders as he worked. He turned, swiped the back of a leather-gloved hand across his forehead. He was attractive, she had to admit it. But not in the youthful way Phillip had been. This man was at least fifteen years older, a slim version of Garth Brooks with his almost-shaved haircut and close-clipped goatee.

He bent to grasp two more boards, tipping his head to expose his crown. Abby felt a smile twist the corners of her mouth. Listening to her father replay the work done around their house by Guy Hardy for almost two weeks was wearing thin. Just like his hair. The discovery coaxed a chuckle that got her over the emotional moment. She turned back to her laundry, tossed the folded load into a plastic hamper and carried it across the oak floor into her bedroom.

As she did every weekend, she tucked clean clothes into drawers and opened her closet to hang her few dresses. Today she indulged her nostalgic mood a bit longer, taking a moment to admire the trophies on her top shelf. She trailed fingertips over a shiny engraved surface.

Barrel Racing Champion, High School Women's Division.

Those were better days, long gone. She pressed the door closed on her memories and turned back to the hallway and her list of chores.

As she passed Dillon's room, a quick glance confirmed he was still enjoying his morning nap, snuggled with Cookie Monster for company. Envious of his carefree slumber, she crept past his crib decorated with *Sesame Street* characters, flipped on the radio monitor and hooked it to the waistband of her favorite cutoff jeans. She pulled the door closed and headed for the dishes that perpetually waited in the kitchen. Through the sheer curtains above the sink, the men outside were visible.

Her daddy actually smiled, tilted his head back, clearly enjoying a private joke with his newfound helper. Abby tried to make out the words they exchanged. Even as she identified the feeling in the pit of her stomach, she knew it was unfair. Resentment. She resented the common ground the two had found. If her daddy regaled her with one more tale of their shared accomplishments, she'd cut loose with a scream that would send the neighbor's dog running for cover.

She squashed the thought, knowing she should be grateful. Each time her dad most needed a distraction, Guy seemed to show up. But somehow that didn't sit well with her.

She turned both taps on full force and slipped her hands into bright yellow latex gloves. A squirt of lemon-scented soap produced a mound of bubbles. Some sprung free, floated above the water and danced on the gentle breeze from the fan overhead. The one Guy had hung.

A loud sigh escaped as Abby dragged the back of her forearm across her face to move sweat-dampened curls out of her eyes. Several heavy thumps on the steps outside preceded the creak of the garage door as it opened into the kitchen. She didn't look up from her sudsy work.

"Good morning, Abby." His friendly greeting seemed hesitant, as if he worried about intruding.

Good, he needed to respect her space. It was Saturday, the only day she had to be home alone with her men. She was busy, and she acknowledged again, bummed. Not at all in the mood for an interruption.

"Sorry to interrupt," he apologized. "I see you're busy."

Her head snapped up, eyes wide. Had she actually muttered that last thought out loud or was mind reading another one of his talents? Either way, it was creepy, which only seemed to agitate already sensitive nerves.

"Shorty would like a refill and I offered to get it for him."

She turned to see Guy holding out her dad's favorite mug.

"Mom would have cut his caffeine off hours ago, but I don't see what it can hurt." She angled her head toward the percolator where a red light blinked indicating the pot was still hot.

Guy leaned in the door, and set the mug on a nearby countertop. He tugged off his boots before stepping foot inside the kitchen, white crew socks peeking beneath his snug jeans.

"Backyard's a little muddy after yesterday's rain," he explained.

She should appreciate his courtesy, but she clung to her martyrdom like a security blanket, turned her eyes back to the suds.

"Where's Junior?"

"Napping. And it's Dillon. He's not named after his father," she corrected, more sharply than necessary, sounding for all the world like her mother.

"Sorry," Guy apologized. "It's just the tag we use for the firstborn. Some days my oldest sister actually prefers Junior to her given name. It's quite a mouthful."

"And her name would be…?" She took the bait.

"Martha Elizabeth Meg Hardy-Waverly."

"I agree. That is a mouthful."

"My folks come from big families where it's customary to pay tribute by recycling names. So all of us got saddled with a heavy load. The good news is we only tend to hear them back home."

"And back home is…?" Abby waited, wondering why in the world she was encouraging a conversation she didn't want.

"Keokuk, Iowa. The geode capital of the world."

"Excuse me?" She rested her wrists against the edge of the sink and turned to him, an eyebrow cocked in question.

"You know, those lumpy round rocks with quartz crystals inside." He expanded his chest with exaggerated pride. "It's our state rock."

She had to give in to a small smile. "You're kidding, right?"

"No, way." He shook his head. "We even have a special celebration called…and I'm serious about this…Rocktober Fest. To join the hunt, you have to register and get a permit."

"To find *rocks?*"

"Hey, these are cool, thousands of years old. I'll get some for Dillon." Guy poured coffee into the mug marked #1 Grandpa and padded in his socks across the kitchen floor to the refrigerator.

Then he poured just the right amount of milk and added a half teaspoon of sugar from the bowl on the table. He'd obviously done it before when she wasn't around, knew exactly how her daddy took his coffee. She looked away, the brief smile fading as she attacked a well-worn cast-iron skillet with a scouring pad. Something about the simple but familiar act of fixing that cup of coffee was a little stab to her heart. She should be doing that. But the truth was she couldn't be everywhere at once no matter how hard she tried and she really could use some time off.

"Abby, how would you feel about me taking Shorty to visit your mom this evening? Just to give you a little break."

Was he reading her mind, *again?* Doubtful.

"My daddy's been talking, hasn't he?"

"Nonstop." She heard the chuckle in Guy's voice. "But I enjoy his company so I don't mind. He misses your mother something fierce and I think it helps him to talk about her, about you."

She scrubbed harder.

"You're going to wear the bottom off that thing," he observed.

"Yeah, well, it won't get clean just sitting in the sink."

"So, what do you say about tonight?"

"No, thanks. Mama's expecting me and I don't dare disappoint her."

Dillon's wakeup wail echoed from the monitor on her waistband. He'd never been one to rouse quietly or be content to lie in his crib and amuse himself. Not her son. The instant he was fully awake, he demanded attention.

"Let me get him," Guy offered, sitting the mug on the table, turning toward the door.

"No," Abby insisted. Even though the man meant well, he was making himself entirely too handy. The kind of handy her folks could get attached to. The kind of attachment that would lead to heartbreak once he was gone. And Abby knew that kind of heartbreak all too well.

"Take my daddy his coffee. I'll get Dillon." She peeled off the rubber gloves, tossed them in the dish rack and brushed past Guy.

Dillon stopped his blubbering the instant she appeared. A wobbly smile creased the small face that was perpetually absent of tears.

"You little stinker," she muttered against his soft head as she stepped into his waiting arms and lifted him from the crib. "You're so sure I'll come running that you haven't bothered with real tears since you were a newborn."

She'd read somewhere that a person teaches others how to treat them. It was true. She'd taught everyone in her life to depend upon her to the point of taking her for granted. They'd also learned she'd toe the line no matter the circumstances out of fear of disapproval. How perplexing that when somebody like Guy stepped in to help, she resented it. It was crazy. A self-inflicted, double-edged sword.

Something had to give.

"Guy?"

Above the whir of the circular saw, he heard her call his name. He cut the power and slid the protective goggles up to his forehead. Tipping his head back, he took in the vision of Abby Cramer in a quick sweep that he hoped didn't make him seem like a frat boy. Worn sneakers, bare legs, frayed and faded jean shorts, and a loose Texas Longhorns T-shirt. A riot of wild blond curls surrounded a face enchantingly pink from her work in the warm kitchen.

Wow, she's adorable.

"Is that offer to give Dad a lift to the hospital this evening still good?"

"Sure is." Guy had made other plans when she'd turned him down hours earlier, but he could shift some things around to free up the time. He was glad for the chance to check for himself on Sarah Reagan's progress. Still, he was amazed Abby had changed her mind. Shorty had said she wouldn't go for the offer and he wasn't surprised when his daughter shot down the request.

Guy stood, stretching the kinks out of his long legs while effectively removing the potential for another glance at hers. "Is anything wrong?"

"No, I just realized I was looking a gift horse in the mouth."

"Well, I guess a gift horse is certainly an improvement over a horse's behind," he couldn't resist teasing.

Her gaze dropped. "So you *did* hear that the other day. Sorry." She nudged a little pile of sawdust between the boards to the grass below. "And I apologize about my grumpy mood earlier."

"Hey, everybody's allowed to have a bad day now and again." Boy, had living in a house full of women ever taught him that. As well as *never* to make that observation out loud unless he wanted a punch to his gut.

"Thanks for letting me off the hook." Her gaze met his. "But I don't deserve it. If Mama heard me being ungracious in her kitchen, she'd send me to my room without dinner."

He smiled at the thought, realizing there was probably more than a kernel of truth in the statement. By all observation, the mistress of this house ran a tight ship and that included the crew as well as the vessel.

"I personally think you should go shopping instead of to your room."

Her brows pulled together as she seemed to consider his suggestion. From the appealing way she puckered her lips as she thought, he guessed shopping was not the stress reliever of choice for Abby that it was for members of the gaggle.

"As tempting as that sounds, I have a dozen phone calls to make before my playground committee meeting tomorrow so I think I'll catch up on that. I'm working with the Mother's-Day-Out group to build a playground. Our funds are limited so we're doing the landscaping ourselves with used railroad timbers and buying secondhand equipment a piece at a time when we run across it on sale. It's slow going but everybody pitches in when they can."

"Sounds like a great bunch of folks. After your committee stuff tomorrow do you want to make a run out to Lake Travis with me? Your dad says he had a favorite largemouth spot up there at one time and you know how to find it."

"You're a bass rat?" She squinted, looked at him differently, like he'd finally said something that might be of interest to her.

"I was raised on the Mississippi, fished every chance I got just to get away from my sisters."

"They didn't fish?"

"Casey did." Of course. "But I haven't fished in freshwater for years. I mostly compete in tournaments offshore when I work a job on the coast. Which is why I can't wait to get down to Galveston on the next site."

Abby smiled. A real smile that plumped her cheeks and lit her cocoa-brown eyes. "That sounds like so much fun. I used to go with Daddy all the time but we haven't been in several years."

Guy already knew that. Knew lots of stuff he probably shouldn't, but there was no stopping Shorty when he was in the mood to talk about his baby girl.

"Then it's a deal?" Guy offered his hand.

"Deal." She gave him a quick, no-nonsense shake, jammed her hands into the hip pockets of her cutoffs and turned back to the house.

The screen door banged behind her. With a shudder Guy realized he'd almost said *date* instead of *deal*. Shorty had dropped a warning, the mention of dating around Abby was a waste of breath. Something to be avoided at all cost.

As if Guy hadn't recognized the challenge by the cagey old daddy that his daughter wouldn't agree to a date with the owner of Heart and Home in a hundred years, anyway.

CHAPTER FIVE

ABBY'S NOSE TWITCHED. Guy smelled so nice.

Like lumber and leather and lemon oil. Which made perfectly good sense considering he spent most of his time in a store that sold those things.

A trip to the lake was not a bad way to spend a car ride after a busy day of meetings.

To focus on something other than how amazing Guy smelled, she thought about the recently planted beds of blooming day lilies. Their playground effort was starting to become visible. There was a metal frame donated by the salvage shop where new swings would eventually hang, a dome-shaped network of monkey bars that needed sanding and fresh paint, and a low fence surrounding a two-year-old pecan tree planted in Phillip's memory.

An embarrassing flush seeped throughout her body. Her palms grew moist as her face went hot with shame. The playground would be a tribute to the selfless young man who'd willingly given his very life so the children in another country might experience the freedom his son would likely take for granted.

Phillip, her dearest friend, had made the ultimate sacrifice and here she was, admiring the scent of another man.

What is wrong with me? I have enough shortcomings without adding lustfulness to the list.

Guy heard Abby's sigh from the passenger seat. Something stirred inside him. He didn't want to call it envy. Envy was longing for what someone else had. He had a close relationship with his own parents so that couldn't be it.

Was it protectiveness? No, he'd felt that for the gaggle all his life. Was used to it, had been defending a sister's honor or helping out a wannabe girlfriend for as long as he could remember. That wasn't it. Still, something niggled at him, something to do with Abby.

She was different from the women he'd casually dated or the Hardy girls who were self-

confident and secure. They'd had their share
of worry what with their mom's Parkinson's
and their dad's bypass surgery, but there were
a slew of them to stick together. Abby was
alone, vulnerable in ways that a big family
couldn't relate to. But she appeared not to notice, even determined not to let him help her
the way most women in his life naturally did.

It had been "Guy to the rescue!" for as long
as he could remember. It was gratifying, like
his habit of giving blood once a month. He
liked it, took pride in doing good deeds. And
he realized with a wry smile that it was bug-
ging him no end to accept that Abby Cramer
didn't much want his services or advice. In
fact, she was still questioning his motives as
the store owner, no matter what he'd said to
reassure her. Smart cookie. Guy's gut stirred
again, this time with guilt. She had reason to
remain suspicious but he was on a mission to
change that.

He glanced down at the freshly buffed toes
of his boots, his mind casting back to the previous evening. Abby had been on the tele-
phone when he'd returned for Shorty. She
hadn't even looked up from the notes she'd

been taking on a yellow pad by the kitchen sink, had just waved over her shoulder and continued her phone conversation when her father had called goodbye.

The trip to the rehab center had been an enlightening one, but all time spent with Shorty was informational. The irascible old fella had been confined to his wheelchair with limited access to his own house and community for so long that he was starved for conversation. Well, you couldn't exactly call it conversation since it was mostly one-sided, with Shorty sharing tales of his life and his two womenfolk. Guy had already heard more about Abby's marriage to Phillip Cramer than he had a right to know. He cringed imagining how angry Kate or Andrea would be if their father rattled off personal stories about their husbands the way Shorty did about Phillip.

What had he said just last night about the boy being so shy he could hardly string three words together without stammering? "But being around my baby girl caused the knot to slip right out of that kid's tongue. Why, he would talk for hours to Abby without tripping over a *T* or being snared by an *S*."

Shorty had grumbled aloud on several occasions over the past couple of weeks that he hoped his daughter would find a "grown man" to take care of her and Dillon the next time around. Then he'd leveled dark eyes at Guy and added, "But not anytime soon."

The unnecessary warning was loud and clear.

But Guy had dodged entanglements for thirty-eight years and had no intention of a committed relationship at this juncture in his life. There were stores to open, board members, foreign investors and stockholders to answer to, plenty of family to care for without being saddled with one of his own. In short, his life was full and he was happy. No matter how much he sympathized, a woman wasn't part of the plan. And certainly not one so young, caught in the vise between a small child and aging parents.

No, Shorty's cautions weren't needed. Guy had a plan, and work to do that would protect Hearth and Home. He'd made progress with Shorty and even Sarah had invited him to sit in the chair beside her bed and tell her all about his family. That just left Abby.

He'd win her over if it was the last thing he did. And he had to do it before Casey showed up and started crowding him.

As usual.

ABBY'S COMMITTEE MEETING had dragged on forever. It was almost noon when she'd called to say she was free. Then after he'd arrived at the house, she'd kept him waiting in the driveway while she no doubt gave a long list of instructions to the H&H employee who'd volunteered to spend the afternoon with Dillon and Shorty.

Now, with the sun high overhead in a brilliant blue Texas canopy they headed northwest, left the traffic-congested city limits of Austin behind and picked up the trail of the Colorado River. According to Abby, Travis was the longest of the Texas Highland Lakes, winding its way for over sixty miles through the famed Hill Country. The drive was leisurely and breathtaking, as they marveled over views of the pristine water and surrounding hills.

She hugged the passenger's door of the SUV, her window rolled down, a glow of pleasure on her face. Her head was poked out, wild curls flapping in the breeze reminding him of a blond cocker spaniel. The thought of making that comparison out loud zipped through his mind and he squashed it like a bug on the windshield.

"Mansfield Dam is over there." She turned to him long enough to motion several miles across the view. "Travis was created in the late 1930's when they dammed up the Colorado. She has almost three hundred miles of shoreline, just over two hundred feet at the deepest point." Abby continued her travelogue, ticking off facts about the manmade system.

"You know a little something about this place, don't you?" He stated the obvious.

"I know a lot about it. I did an environmental project on the lake system while I was at the University of Texas."

"So you researched all that information?"

"I already knew most of it." She swept her arm, palm up, toward the waters before them. "This is my neck of the woods. Daddy and I love it up here and he taught me the history of the lake while we sat in a boat together for hours on end."

"You must miss it."

"Mostly I miss Daddy the way he used to be," her voice dropped, so low he barely heard the next. "But I miss a lot of things."

She was quiet for a long while, her gaze fixed on the sparkling surface of the lake, probably remembering better days before the insidious disease had claimed Shorty's mobility. More than likely thinking about those other things she missed.

Her husband. Phillip.

Guy felt a twinge of jealousy. He dropped his left elbow to the open window ledge, squeezed the wheel with his right hand, feeling like pond scum at the thought. What kind of jerk would be even the least bit envious of a woman's late husband? Especially since that jerk had no interest in the woman, even if she did seem more appealing each time he was with her.

"But all of that was a long time ago." She sounded resigned. "Life goes on whether we want it to or not." She turned her face his way and offered him a small smile that did little to disguise the sadness in her eyes.

His chest tightened. They needed something to lift the somber mood threatening to settle between them like a stone dropping through the crystal waters. As much as the women in his life complained about the calorie consumption afterward, food was always a good distraction. He slowed as the road drew to a fork. There was a gas station to the right where they could get bottled water and maybe some fruit.

"I could use a snack, how about you?"

She studied the road ahead as she nodded agreement, then pointed to the left. "There's a little mobile unit not too far up that way. I haven't been there for a couple of years but it's always been a favorite spot on this side of the lake so I'm sure it's still there. You game for a most excellent corn dog? You might even have heard of the owner. He did a little track and field back in his day."

Guy's interest was piqued, but it also happened that as a kid he'd choked on a bite of corn dog and hadn't been able to stomach the thought of the deep fried excuse for meat on a stick in years. But if the lady wanted one...

"Sure," he agreed.

Mobile unit was a fancy way of saying vintage, no, make that decrepit, Airstream trailer surrounded by an awful multicolored picket fence. The menu, painted in sprawling red letters on a sheet of white plywood boasted Curbo's Fine Dining! The Fastest Food South of the Mason-Dixon! Since everything about Texas was purported to be the biggest and grandest, it was often difficult for an outsider to know what was the real deal and what was tongue-in-cheek. As Guy cut the engine of the truck, he suspected the latter description was about to be applied to this roadside dining experience.

ABBY JUMPED TO THE GROUND and slammed the passenger door as a wave of déjà vu crashed over her senses. How many times had she stood in this same spot, felt the afternoon sun on her face, the constant lake breeze stirring her curls? Her stomach growled for a greasy corn dog or a paper cup overflowing with chili cheese fries. She tucked her fingers into the hip pockets of her tight Levi's and strode toward the window.

"Danny, are you in there?" She called.

A physically fit fifty-something man with close-cropped gray hair appeared at the opening. A wide smile spread across a ruddy face as he angled his head back and squinted through the rimless glasses balanced low on the bridge of his nose.

"Well, as I live and struggle for breath. Sport, would you look at what the tide washed up?" He reached to open the trailer's small door and a long-legged, Italian greyhound bounded down the three wooden steps. Abby knelt, one knee pressed to the crushed-shale surface of the parking lot, as the aging pet smothered her cheek with wet greetings.

"Abby Reagan, is that really you?"

"It's me, Danny. But it's been Abby Cramer for a while now."

"Don't tell me that shy Cramer boy actually worked up the nerve to talk you into marrying him," Danny teased as he took the steps in a single stride and moved toward her, arms outstretched.

She continued to smile as she stepped into

his gentle hug, knowing what was coming next but not wanting to dampen the mood of their reunion. "Yes, he did but Phillip and I were only married for a few months before his active reserves unit was deployed to Iraq. He was killed in an insurgent attack outside of Baqouba almost two years ago."

The older man stilled, folded her tight and she felt him press a gentle kiss to the top of her head. "I'm so sorry for your loss, little girl."

"Thanks," she murmured against his chest, aware of how long it had been since her own father had been able to hug her with such comfort. "But we have a beautiful son to show for our short marriage so Phillip will always be part of my life."

Boots crunched on the road nearby and Abby remembered Guy. She gave Danny a quick squeeze before stepping away to make introductions.

"Guy, this is Danny Curry, known to the locals as Curbo."

"And the reason for that is duly noted," Guy said with an easy grin as he extended his hand. "Sir, I'd know Curbo the Turbo any-where!"

"You're too kind. That was a lot of years ago." Danny dipped his chin modestly.

"Not long enough to forget the Texas Turbo that was on my Wheaties box when I was a kid."

He remebered watching the running phe-nomenon become the pride of the U.S.A. team at one Olympic games where he'd won three gold medals and set a world-record time in the eight-hundred-meter event.

"It's an honor to meet you. Guy Hardy of Hearth and Home."

"You must be Keith Hardy's son. You're a long way from Iowa."

"Ahh, you're familiar with us." Guy nod-ded, the crinkle of a smile at the corners of his eyes indicating he was clearly pleased by the name recognition, especially in this com-pany.

"I've had H&H in my stock portfolio since you went public," Danny confirmed. "Glad to see you expanding into the South."

"We've just opened our first Texas super center, near Barton Springs and South Lamar."

"Nice piece of real estate." Danny's eyes widened. "You should do well there. I need to get into town soon to check it out. I could use some new patio furniture." He gestured beyond the trailer. Guy followed the direction Danny pointed and sucked in a breath at the sight of an enormous home built of limestone block, set well back off the road. Miles of white fence surrounded the lakefront acreage, a well-appointed boat dock visible from their vantage point.

"I see corn dogs are a booming business!"

Abby grinned behind her hand, enjoying Guy's response to the humble front Danny placed on his thriving entrepreneurial business and his senior partnership in the Emerald Point Marina.

"I can't complain." He turned to her. "Tell me the latest on your folks. You and your dad used to be weekend regulars and we haven't seen you up here in a coon's age."

"That's because Dad's confined to a wheelchair, now."

"The MS?"

"Yep." She nodded. "The bad days began to outweigh the good ones and he couldn't trust his legs anymore, so he had to accept full-time use of the chair. He's adjusted about as well as you'd expect."

Danny snorted. "That old coot, adjust to life in a wheelchair? Bet that went over like a rock in the butter beans."

"Exactly!" She laughed at the native Texan who was also known for his command of Southern colloquialisms. "But we've made some minor alterations to the house so he gets around pretty well."

"I'm guessing if you're not fishing then you don't get to rodeo much these days either."

GUY'S ATTENTION SHIFTED from the sight of the incredible lakefront property before him back to Abby.

Rodeo?

What was that all about? He watched her soft curls bob as her chin dropped and she shook her head.

"There hasn't been time or money for barrel racing in years." She tilted her head back to see into the taller man's eyes; a wistful smile flickered at the corners of her lips. "But it's nice that you remember."

"It's not likely I'd forget after all the bragging your dad used to do about your rankings. He thought you could have gone pro. And I always suspected you were an urban cowgirl at heart. Matter of fact, I thought maybe this hardware-store cowboy was your beau." He angled his head downward and cocked an eyebrow, obviously a reference to Guy's boots. Boots in Texas seemed to be a functional thing. Guy was starting to feel guilty that his were only about fashion and comfort.

"Oh, no." Abby shook her head vigorously, a little too much so for Guy's ego. Was it *that* bad having somebody think she might actually be with him voluntarily?

CHAPTER SIX

"MR. HARDY AND I are only acquainted because Mama fell and broke her hip in his store and he's been helping Dad around the house while she recovers." Abby turned wide brown eyes on Guy.

"Is that a fact?" Danny narrowed his dark gaze and shifted his weight toward the subject of his examination. "So you're just staying close out of professional duty?"

The two waited for a response from Guy.

He felt like a stink bug trapped under a jelly jar. Scrutiny was one thing, but the look on the Texas Turbo's face was bordering something akin to suspicion. Guy's polo-style shirt began to feel uncomfortably snug and warm. He was definitely not accustomed to experiencing heat for that purpose. Especially since it was being ignited by Abby herself.

First she'd been emphatic that there was nothing personal between them, then she'd called him *Mister* for crying out loud, and now she'd gotten this man who was infamous for his aggressively competitive nature on high alert. Was there even a slim chance he was losing his ability to charm a female? Guy really needed a gaggle check. He could hear Casey cackling already, especially when she learned it was Curbo the Turbo impatiently jangling keys at her brother.

"Quite honestly, sir, it started as professional concern, but the Reagans are a wonderful family. It's a pleasure to be around them."

Danny straightened. The furrows between his eyes relaxed.

"In that case..." He pulled the set from the front right pocket of his well-worn jeans. Without notice he tossed the keys skyward. Guy scooped them from the air, grasping the fish-shaped foam object that would keep the set afloat if dropped overboard.

Danny continued, "...Take this little lady for a boat ride. I have a feeling it's something she needs, whether she'll admit it or not." He beamed affectionately at Abby and the smile of gratitude she returned made Guy's heart ache. This girl really wasn't used to people doing nice things for her, something the women in his life had long taken for granted.

"That really isn't necessary." She tried to sound convincing, but the adorable flush of anticipation that rushed into her cheeks said otherwise.

"It's not only necessary, it's an order. Take the woody." He pointed toward the dock. "She's got a full tank and you'll find bait and everything else you need in the boathouse." He nodded at Guy. "I won't take no for an answer so get her out of here before she makes the effort."

Danny turned and with the greyhound at his heels walked twenty paces to a wide entrance in the white fence, removed the padlock and swung the gate open.

"What about our corn dogs?" Abby asked, her bottom lip protruding in a fake pout.

"Help yourself." He motioned toward the trailer.

Abby bounded up the short row of steps and disappeared inside the ancient trailer. She emerged moments later carrying a brown paper sack bearing several slowly spreading grease spots. Guy reached for the passenger's door of the SUV as he imagined the havoc the days-old cooking oil would play with his digestive system.

But the look of pure pleasure on Abby's face when she climbed inside clutching the sack made him feel like a heel for his selfish thoughts. She just wanted a little fun away from her life being sandwiched between two demanding generations of family. He returned her grin before he closed the door, feeling the excitement of the moment.

He gave the man rightly dubbed the Texas Turbo a friendly wave as the H&H truck headed down the blacktop road that threaded through acres of Bermuda grass and ended in a small parking area behind the private waterfront home. Guy was impressed to find a thirty-eight-foot tournament fishing boat powered by triple Mercury 275s.

A Chris-Craft Woody Speedster waited in the next slip. The classic teak pleasure craft should have been preserved in a showroom, not floating serenely in the waters of Lake Travis. Guy hesitated, wondering if he should remove his boots before climbing onboard.

Abby didn't appear too concerned as she

tossed the sack of food on the leather bench seat and then headed for the boathouse where she seemed to know her way around.

"You've done this before, I see," he called as she ducked into the structure large enough to completely enclose several well-appointed boats, plenty of equipment and sported a deck on top with patio furniture and a professional-grade outdoor grill.

Looking for all the world like a female version of Tom Sawyer, she fairly skipped across the wooden planks with one fist clutching a couple of rods, the other swinging a bait well and dip net.

"Yeah, Daddy and Danny used to get on like a barn ablaze. We'd drag our little bass boat up here and stop for a bite to eat and before you knew it he'd have us fishing off the dock, visiting with his family or taking the Jet Skis out for a run. He's quite a business success in these parts but believes in a lot of playtime, too."

"And his primary business these days is *fine fast food?*" Guy crooked an eyebrow in skeptical question.

Abby's laugh was a charming melody that

carried across the slick surface of the water. "That's just what he does to stay plugged in to casual visitors. Danny is the major shareholder of the largest marina on the lake."

Guy whistled appreciation. "Nice to see a great Olympic athlete parlay his fame into a substantial living."

They settled into the beautifully restored boat; Guy cranked the powerful well-tuned engine and eased out into open water. He glanced to his left where Abby hugged her side of the craft as she'd done in the truck. Again he got the sense she was putting as much physical distance as possible between them.

"Where to?" He looked to her for directions.

HER SKIN WARMED beneath the focus of his gaze and she pressed closer to her side of the woody, torn between the excitement of accepting Danny's generosity and the silly nervousness of being alone on the lake with a man. Not a boy. A man. One who seemed more appealing every day. The prickle of gooseflesh shimmied up her spine. She was twenty-four for crying out loud. Hardly a schoolgirl who needed a chaperone in public during broad daylight. So why did she feel so hesitant, still edgy about Guy's intentions?

"Head toward that big rock for about ten minutes." She pointed in the distance to a landmark her dad had taught her to use for navigation. "There's a little cove off to the left. It used to be a perfect spot for white crappy. They're powerful little fighters, fun to catch and release."

He throttled forward and the craft planed out, skimming across the glassy surface that was made to order, reflecting the brilliant blue Texas sky. She slumped down, leaned her head back against the leather seat, her pleasure lightly tinged with guilt. There was so much that needed to be done for Dillon and her school kids, so many things to worry about where her parents were concerned. And here she was taking the afternoon off like she hadn't a care in the world.

For the moment she'd relax and let her cares be blown by the wind that had her hair flapping like the wings of a hummingbird.

She reached up to clutch her curls into submission.

A warm hand closed around her fingers. She jerked free from the unexpected touch and instantly regretted her reaction. It was the first personal contact she'd felt from a man since the morning at the base when she'd held Phillip for the final time.

"Sorry I startled you," Guy apologized, his eyes conveying the same message. "But don't do that. Casey is forever trying to squash her hair into a clip or a ponytail. The truth is curls like you two have are meant to be free so they can be admired."

A glint of mischief sparked in his eyes as she dropped her hands to her lap.

"May I?" He hesitantly reached toward her, indicating he wanted to smooth her hair.

He'd been nothing but a gentleman for weeks. Always supportive, willing to help, never asking for anything in return. In good conscience, how could she still be suspicious? Wouldn't it be wrong to continue to hold his financial and personal status against him, basically what she'd been doing since she'd discovered his identity?

"Sure," she agreed. With his right hand he reduced the speed to a safe cruise in open water then with his left he sifted curls through his fingers. Once, then twice. The second time he lightly brushed her scalp. She tingled from the outside in.

It took half a nanosecond to realize that letting him touch her was a big mistake.

I'm pathetic.

"You're incredible."

Certain he was teasing, she searched his face for humor but saw only appreciation in his azure-blue eyes.

"I have to agree with my daddy, you're a very kind man, Guy Hardy."

"Shorty actually said that?" It was Guy's turn to look suspicious, and with just cause. Praise from her parents was more precious than plutonium and harder to come by.

"Yes."

"About me?"

Yes, about you." She couldn't help smiling at his disbelief.

"I admit hearing Shorty feels that way means a lot, but I didn't compliment you out of kindness. Abby—"

Her face warmed with embarrassment. She waved away his words but he caught her hand, determined to finish what he'd started.

"Abby, while there's no doubt you're a beautiful woman, it's your gift of spirit that makes you so attractive. My sisters are a generous bunch and I love them to distraction. But you may be the most selfless and giving young lady I know."

HE WATCHED HER stare for several long moments, her eyes gleaming, puzzled. As with the first day they met, she seemed reluctant to accept, much less believe, she deserved the kind words. Her gaze fell to their hands. He released hers and she reached for the sack, rustled the contents inside and drew out a golden-brown gob of fried dough affixed to a wooden stick.

"Thank you, Guy," she modestly acknowledged what he'd said. "Now, I'm about to earn those compliments by giving you the first bite."

As she spoke, she ripped open a small packet, squeezed out a crooked line of yellow mustard and then pushed the corn dog in his direction. The motion of her hand didn't slow as she approached his face, leaving no doubt that she expected him to open wide. Feeling a bit like Dillon must when Abby shoveled oatmeal into his mouth whether he wanted it or not, Guy reluctantly parted his lips and awaited the inevitable.

"Oh, get that terrified look off your face. It's a corn dog, not a cow paddy!" she teased. "Be flexible, Guy. Take a bite."

He sank his teeth into the cornmeal-covered hot dog. As he began to chew, he gave a head bob of approval.

"Seeeeee?" she chided.

The burst of spicy mustard, the crispy crunch of the fried shell and the tender bite of all-beef wiener were, to his amazement, a surprisingly nice combination. The fact that he didn't choke was a plus, but would the immediate gratification outweigh the indigestion that was bound to follow?

The trepidation he felt must have shown in his face because Abby's smile drooped over his failure to share her enthusiasm.

He reached across the console, accepted the wooden stick from her, took another large bite and basked in the approval of her broad grin. What was a little grease if it made her that happy?

As she went to work on her own snack, he deftly steered the woody through another boat's foamy wake, continuing toward the landmark rock she'd pointed out.

"Just around that next bend there's a cove off to the left. We can idle in there and drop anchor for a while if you want to wet a hook."

Fifteen minutes later, they stood back to back in companionable silence, casting off opposite sides of the boat. Abby got a hit almost immediately and reeled in a fat perch. Guy watched, impressed as she expertly removed the lure then gently slipped the wriggling fish back into the still water with hardly a ripple to disturb the surface.

He felt a tug, jerked his line, reeled hard and frowned. Snagged, but good. Abby caught sight of his hardship, snorted a burst of laughter.

"Oh, I should have warned you, there are lots of submerged stumps around here."

Bested by a girl. And it wasn't even the Warden!

"That would have been useful information *two minutes ago*." He pretended to be annoyed; she continued to snicker.

At the exact moment he realized there was no additional tackle onboard, his line snapped. He abandoned his useless rod and settled on the Chris-Craft's rear bench seat. The vantage point allowed him to admire Abby's petite but curvy figure encased in snug jeans and a sleeveless T-shirt. The definition in her arms said she did a lot of lifting. The better he knew her, the more he understood she bore the mental heavy lifting for her family as well.

"And now that I have nothing to do, I'm all ears. Tell me about this rodeo career of yours."

Poised to cast her lure into the water, Abby paused while she appeared to consider how to reply. She turned a brief glance his way and seemed satisfied his question was earnest. Then she whipped the tip of her pole forward, releasing the line that arched for fifty feet before meeting the water with a soft *plop*. Guy had been tournament fishing since he was old enough to afford the entry fees, so a textbook cast was an area he knew well and appreciated. He couldn't hold back a smile realizing it was a skill his baby sister hadn't quite mastered.

He recalled Abby's comment that her dad and Curbo got along like a barn on fire. That was the way Abby and Casey were going to be once they were acquainted.

Guy felt his eyes widen, wondering what had prompted such an absurd thought. There was no reason for the two women to meet. Still, setting something up might have merit. They were polar opposites with a lot in common. It had the potential to be a perfect friendship.

Or a disaster. Maybe introducing them was not such a good idea after all.

ABBY MULLED OVER Guy's innocent question. She took her time, reeled slowly, unsure she wanted to probe into an area where the fond memories crowded all her senses and left her longing for the sport she could never again afford. She loved the smell that radiated from the neck of a barrel horse during the heat of a race against the clock. The dust in her nostrils, the grit that inevitably got in her teeth, the constant soreness of her muscles, and the cheer of a familiar crowd were all part of the personal reward of the amateur rodeo circuit.

"Abby? Is the subject off-limits?"

Guy's question snapped her out of her reverie. She angled her body where she could hold a conversation and continue to cast without the sharp hook on the end of her line being a threat to her spectator.

"Not really. It's just something I haven't thought about in ages so I was going through a little memory dump for a moment there."

"Were you as good as Curbo said? Could you have competed professionally?"

She tipped her hand side to side in a so-so gesture. Yes, actually she *was* pretty good but that had been years ago, not something worth bragging about today.

"I had some lucky rides."

"Lucky?" His eyebrows tipped together, his voice skeptical.

"Okay, I was blessed with a little natural talent and some great horses while I was in high school, so I guess I do have a few dusty trophies in the top of my closet to show for it."

She tossed the lure perfectly, appreciated its clean entry into the water. Daddy was going to enjoy hearing the details of this impromptu visit to their favorite spot. He'd love knowing she hadn't lost her touch.

"Did you own horses?"

"No. My part-time job at the arena paid for my tack but it was the kindness of people from our community that kept me on horseback. Rodeo requires a significant investment of time and money and even professionally the prize payoff is pretty slim most of the time. There was never much hope for me to continue once I went to college. Then when Daddy's condition began to deteriorate, it became impossible."

"Where was Phillip during those years?" The tone said he was sincerely interested.

"He was there every minute." Her hands stilled from the business of reeling, her gaze locked with Guy's. "Phillip was my best friend for most of my life. I was his only friend." She ached with the memory. "He was very shy and had a nearly disabling speech impediment when he was nervous. But with me and my family there was no judgment so there was no stammer. He didn't have the same comfort level at his home so he basically grew up at our house."

"And he was the only boy you ever dated?"

"Yeah, I guess that's true. I never even considered seeing anyone else." Not that her parents hadn't suggested it a thousand times. "It would have broken Phillip's heart."

Guy nodded, seemed to understand.

"You are an amazing lady, Abby."

She glanced at her watch and reluctantly stretched her line to attach the lure to an eye near the rod's grip.

"I don't know why you'd say that."

"You're a great mom to Dillon and a devoted daughter, you teach, you fish, you ride and from what little you've let me observe, you volunteer for a half-dozen things, including keeping your husband's memory alive with that playground. Pretty amazing to a guy like me with only one commitment and it's a family business at that. You need to give yourself more credit, sweetheart."

He raised the anchor and she reached shaking hands to coil the rope, using the excuse to turn her face away, not wanting him to see how his endearment was affecting her. Not even wanting to see it herself.

He took his place at the wheel to start the engine.

"And, more importantly," he continued, "give yourself a break before you're dried up and burnt out like that awful toast Dillon cuts his teeth on."

She focused on the truth in what Guy said. A break? What did that mean? And if she followed his advice, would anybody pick up the slack? Of course not.

The sun had ducked behind the clouds. The air was cool. The ride back to Danny's would be a chilly one. Guy reached for the light-weight cotton pullover he'd wisely brought from the truck and tossed into the boat. He handed it to her.

"Here, wear this, Goldilocks. And lean toward me instead of huddling over there like I'm the big bad wolf."

She accepted the soft shirt, tempted to press her face into it, inhale his scent. Instead she looked skeptically at the pullover and recovered with a snappy reply. "You've got your fairy tales mixed up, Papa Bear."

"Oh, hush." He grinned. "And get that look off your face. It's a sweater, not a straight-jacket. Be flexible, Abigail Cramer. Put it on." Guy mimicked her earlier demand with a *got-cha* glint in his eyes.

She returned his easy smile and snuggled into the warmth of the sweater that embraced her like a soul mate's hug.

Perfectly.

And as she did she inhaled. Lumber, leather and lemon oil.

Guy.

CHAPTER SEVEN

"MONDAYS ARE CRAZY," Abby muttered to herself. "I shouldn't have let Guy talk me into this."

She swung her six-year-old Civic into the Hearth and Home parking lot, cut the engine and ticked off the must-do list for the afternoon and evening. This was the first stop after leaving school because she'd agreed to meet him to look at bathroom fixtures. He had some ideas about making the private area of her parent's home more user-friendly for a wheelchair and a walker. There was no money for such an industrious project but Guy didn't know it, and there was no harm in listening to the ideas he seemed intent on sharing. The work had to be done eventually, so she might as well know the cost and labor requirements up front.

Mama would be released in a few weeks, hopefully in time for Mother's Day, the date set aside to celebrate the playground dedication.

Abby covered her mouth as a yawn escaped. Each deadline in the coming weeks was dependent upon at least two others and the weight of what had to be accomplished was costing precious sleep. Fortunately the primary need in her projects was time and elbow grease, not cash. But the small band of volunteers was shrinking as the end of the school year approached and the afternoon spring activities morphed into full-time summer commitments.

Each call from a harried mother who had to back out of planting or painting left Abby to do the work. It was either that or abandon some part of the playground, not an acceptable option. What Dillon would think in ten years of the efforts his mother made today mattered a great deal. She wanted to give her son a special place, beyond a box in the attic, where he could feel connected to his father. And maybe one day it would also become a place where she could release Phillip once and for all.

A shrill *beep, beep, beep* caught her attention as a forklift backed out of the H&H commercial dock door, prepared to deposit a load of treated lumber onto the flatbed delivery vehicle. The logo on the truck was the same on the shirts the employees wore. It was becoming a comforting sight. Kinda like Guy.

"Hey, Abby!" Leah, the store manager called a greeting from the courtesy desk as Abby entered through the wide double doors. "How's Mrs. Reagan?"

"She's responding very well to her physical therapy, thanks for asking."

Leah rounded the counter and closed the space between them. "That's wonderful news." She embraced Abby loosely and patted her shoulder in that comforting touch Texans love. "Please give your sweet mama our best and tell her the staff is praying for her to make a full recovery. And if there's anything we can do for you, just holler."

"Thanks, Leah, but y'all have been incredible already, bringing meals and helping out with Dillon and my daddy."

"Hey, that's what a community is for, and one of the things that most appeals to me about working here. It's a family atmosphere and the Hardys believe in taking care of their employees as well as customers. I think it's the main reason they recovered after that nasty lawsuit a couple of years back."

Abby knew nothing about a legal battle, but filed that unexpected piece of information away to be investigated when she had a spare minute.

"Would you happen to know where I can find Mr. Hardy? He asked me to stop by to look at some bathroom hardware." She felt the need to explain.

"Sure, Guy said you'd be in. He's waiting in the office." She pointed toward the stairs. "Go on up."

Abby climbed the steps and knocked lightly on the door marked Private.

"It's open, Abby," the familiar voice called, obviously expecting her.

Inside the dimly lit room, Guy sat with his back to the door, facing a bank of security monitors. Each flat-panel screen displayed a different area of the store fed by cameras throughout the facility. He seemed to study one in particular, focusing on several shoppers in a busy aisle.

"If I've come at a bad time I might be able to drop by later in the week."

He swiveled the high-backed leather chair, giving her his attention. Her gaze locked on his engaging bluebonnet eyes. The smile that spread across his handsome face caused the strangest flutter in her belly, not unlike the feel of Dillon's cartwheels during the months she'd carried him beneath her heart.

"Nonsense. I'm glad you're here. I've got a lot of stuff to show you."

He twisted a knob on his desk lamp, throwing a wash of bright light across the work surface. As he busied himself unrolling a sheet of drawings, she noted the calendar. An orange line was drawn to highlight several weeks, ending with a double circle around Mother's Day.

A thoughtful son. Again her insides danced.

He swept his hand to indicate the blueprints. She leaned forward, taking a close look at the sketch of her parents' bathroom, both before and after Guy's ideas. Impressive.

She hesitated, not sure how to continue. With the strength of the Hardy family resources behind him, he might not understand her financial constraints. And while living on a budget so tight that every dollar counted was nothing to be ashamed of, it was a bit embarrassing to have to explain.

"Guy, listen," she said, searching for the right words. "It's great that you want to show me your ideas, and I'd love to be able to do this stuff for my mom and dad someday, but we don't have the money just now for new fixtures, much less structural changes, something you've probably never had to worry about." She straightened, took a step away from the drawings that were luxurious daydreams.

He reached for the other executive-style chair in the room, rolled it close to his and opened his palm in an invitation. She hesitated, considering whether or not to sit. He grasped her fingers and tugged her down to the soft leather seat.

"There." She heard satisfaction in his voice. "One less decision for you to worry about today."

She returned his grin, appreciating that he realized how much was perpetually on her plate.

"Now, let me clear something up for you and put your mind at rest at least on this subject." He scooted his chair close, their knees brushed lightly. A pleasant warmth tingled. She considered backing up a bit but the kind squint of his eyes told her his closeness was to share something personal.

"Obviously the Hardy clan is financially well off, but it wasn't always that way. Both of my parents came from very big families. Dad had seven brothers and sisters, Mom had nine. With that many kids to feed and clothe there was always a struggle to make ends meet, so they each grew up in extremely frugal households. That experience drove the way they raised us, even after the business took off. To give you an idea, my mom only has a few dogmatic rules but one of them is that none of her kids are ever to go out in public in sneakers."

"Are you serious?"

"As a copperhead's bite." His brows tipped together as he nodded, leaving no doubt. "Mother was the fifth daughter so she wore hand-me-down shoes till she left home at nineteen. All they could afford were sneakers and by the time a pair made it to her it would be in pretty rough shape. But used clothes and shoes were just a fact of life back then so she wore them without complaint. Still, she made up her mind that her kids would never have to be embarrassed by old tennis shoes in public, the way she was."

"So, I guess she refuses to wear them today, huh?"

"Oh, sneakers are a symbol of *family* to her, to all of us. When we go to my parents' house, that's all we wear. It's our way of connecting to her personal experience, saying we're home, the most special place in our hearts. But away from the house we wear 'Sunday-go-to-meeting shoes' as my chubby, white-haired grandma Hazel used to say."

Guy slid up one pant leg and admired the hand-tooled exotic leather roper that had set him back at least a thousand dollars.

"I just happen to be partial to boots so this is my way of splurging to celebrate each of our new locations. I buy a pair at the beginning of a project and when it's successful, I fit the boots with cedar shoe trees and retire them to the display rack in my closet."

"How many pairs do you have?" She felt the smallest surge of pleasure at this personal insight he was sharing. It was confirmation she'd been correct the day before. It wasn't right to go on being distrustful of Guy and his family just because instinct told her to be suspicious.

He pressed his lips together and scrunched his brow in concentration as he touched the pad of his right thumb to the tip of each finger, counting to himself.

"Eleven." It was a one-word confession, his expression contrite.

"You don't have to apologize."

"I know, but it almost sounds wasteful considering what I just told you about my parents' upbringing. And given the fact that your boots say you're a rodeo regular where mine say I'm 'all hat and no horse.'"

She smiled at the words her dad often used to tease Guy and reached her hand toward his knee, lightly brushing his dark jeans. The intensity in his eyes said he realized the touch emphasized what she was about to say.

"Guy, I've seen for myself these past few weeks that you're good to other people. You deserve to give yourself a break when it comes to a little luxury in life."

Before she could remove her hand, he closed his over the top of it, gently pressing so she wouldn't withdraw.

"I hope you realize what you just said applies even more to you, Abby. You work so hard to take care of everybody in your life. Not that a new toilet and some non-skid tile in your parents' bathroom are luxuries, but those things will make your life easier, so please let me do this for you. I promise the work will be finished by the day we bring your mother home."

A new toilet and non-skid tile. She'd been hoping that one day a special man would want to share the desires of her heart. This wasn't exactly what she'd had in mind, but it was Guy's way of sharing and there was a quirky sort of intimate quality to it that couldn't be denied.

"It's the least H&H can do," he added.

Scratch that intimate stuff. It was about the store after all and she was a fool to imagine otherwise. Time to be practical, an area where Guy was clearly the expert.

She slid her hand from beneath his and brushed away an errant curl that had flopped across her forehead.

"Accepting your charity will bruise my mother's pride, and I'm sure she'd turn down your offer if we gave her the chance," Abby said with a sigh, resigning herself to do so anyway. "But my realistic side tells me how much my folks would enjoy the comforts and peace of mind and Daddy will love the activity. So I'm going to agree."

"Awesome!"

His face lit with pleasure. Over installing a new commode! The guy really got a kick out of the strangest things.

"And will you also agree to let me do the same for the playground? I can have all new equipment delivered and send out some landscape artists to finish the gardens."

"Absolutely not." She stood, physically drawing the line on his bizarre sense of generosity. "The playground isn't about money, or convenience or even meeting a deadline. This is something I need to do myself. For my son. For my husband."

GUY FELT THE MUSCLES in his face droop; his spirits sagged as well. Of course she wouldn't want his involvement in a project that was a labor of devotion for the husband she would always love. Would a woman ever care for him with her whole heart that way? And if one did, could he trust her motives? Probably no more than Abby seemed willing to trust his right now.

"I'm sorry," he apologized. "My sister Andrea reminded me not too long ago that I get caught up in the details of getting things done and forget the spirit of why I'm doing it."

Confusion and disappointment had to be written all over his face. Feeling like a fool, he turned back to the screens, pretended to scan the various camera angles.

A light touch warmed his shoulder.

"I didn't mean to offend you, Guy." She used the tone reserved for soothing Dillon. How appropriate for a man who was constantly asked by his mother when he would grow up and have a committed relationship.

"No offense taken." Yeah, right. He busied himself with the screens.

He punched the zoom function of a camera

to close in on the activity of a wide row prom-
inently marked with a large Aisle Six sign. A
young couple compared the used hardware in
the man's hand to similar new items on the
display rack. A few feet farther down the row,
a lone figure in overalls, T-shirt and a base-
ball cap adjusted the backpack slung over her
shoulder and positioned large dark glasses
over her eyes. It was difficult to know the
gender for sure, but the slight build and a few
long tufts of hair spilling from beneath the
cap indicated a female shopper.

If you could call what she was doing shopping.

"Check it out." Guy touched the screen,
drawing Abby's attention. The female lifted
something small from the display rack and
awkwardly tucked it into the pocket of her
baggy pants. "I can't believe she's doing this
again." His voice resonated with aggravation.

He stood, paced the office several times
while he clenched and unclenched his fists
and decided what to do. "I'm fed up and about
to put a stop to this once and for all." He
opened the office door and extended his open
palm in an invitation for Abby to join him.

"I'll walk you to the front of the store and then I have to attend to this problem."

"You're going to apprehend that shoplifter yourself?" Her pitch rose. "But isn't that why you employ a security guard? Guy, please don't do anything dangerous."

He enjoyed the way Abby's eyes widened with worry about his safety. Again an odd sense of comfort over her attention squeezed his heart, immediately followed by a selfish pang for giving her reason to be concerned.

"Not to worry. A certain amount of this comes with the territory of retail ownership. Unfortunately I have a lot of experience in this area and it's more unpleasant than anything else. I'll just give this clown enough time to cross the line and then react."

He headed down the steps with Abby close behind.

"Oh, that's right. Once the perpetrator takes the merchandise outside the store they can be apprehended."

He glanced over his shoulder, cocked an eyebrow at the observation. "I see you've been watching those reality cop shows with Shorty," he teased. "Actually you are correct, but I'm more concerned about having room to wrestle this perp to the ground than meeting legal requirements."

At the foot of the stairs he turned and waited.

"Is it okay if I call later?" He qualified the reason for the request. "To check on your folks."

At least he was consistent, Abby thought. Always keeping things professional and practical. But for some reason that was starting to wear thin with her emotions.

"Of course," she assured him.

He took a step closer, the sudden softening around his eyes making him appear for all the world like a man who was about to give her a hug. But instead of opening his arms, he simply extended a hand and lightly touched her elbow.

"I'd walk you to your car, but..."

Her heart dipped at the foolishness of what she'd been imagining. He was politely getting her out of the store so he could attend to business.

She adjusted her purse and searched for her

keys, thankful for an excuse to casually ease away from his contact.

"It's broad daylight and though I'm a natural blonde I can still remember where I left it," she was quick to assure him. She lifted her keys, rattled them in a wave and turned toward the exit.

She slowed just before the motion sensors picked her up and sent the glass doors sliding apart. A glance over her shoulder confirmed Guy was still visible as he moved toward the aisles of merchandise. What he was about to do could be risky. The only way to ease the concern was to see for herself what he was up to. Keeping a careful distance she mirrored his footsteps and watched, determined to see the drama unfold, knowing Daddy would love to hear the replay over dinner.

AS HE APPROACHED aisle six, Guy poked his head around the end cap display. The so-called shopper had evidently completed her selections and was standing in the checkout line, her back to him as he approached. He'd witnessed her amateurish efforts to slip a half-dozen items into her pockets and backpack. None of those were on the black conveyor passing before the store associate now. He had this sorry excuse for a thief dead to rights. This was not only a piece of cake, it would be downright fun.

The clerk accepted payment for the small purchase, wished the customer a pleasant day and handed over the bright orange, recyclable H&H bag. As the woman in overalls approached the door, the wide panes whooshed apart and she stepped across the threshold.

The store security guard approached from another direction. Guy motioned for the guard to stay clear, signaled that the situation was under control.

Without a backward glance, the thief headed across the wide front walk toward the parking lot. Guy moved in on his target, closing the space between them with a few long strides. He made no effort at verbal confrontation. Instead he reached for the woman, grabbed her by the wrist, and as she yelped in surprise he spun her about. He pulled her into his arms, pinned her back against his chest, locking her tight against him with his forearm, his hand over her mouth to silence her.

They exchanged grunts and groans for long moments as his captive flailed about in a vain attempt to break free. The woman's hands waved wildly, she stamped her feet, trying to catch Guy's toe with the heel of her boot. When he loosened his grip to dodge her foot she rammed an elbow into his ribs.

Guy grumbled a threat, pulled the suspect to him and pinned her arms to her sides. With the woman finally subdued, he ducked his head close to her ear and hissed through clenched teeth, "I warned you I was gonna teach you a lesson if you ever tried this again."

She executed an exaggerated shiver at the danger in his tone.

"*You* teach *me* something, hotshot?" The thief's snarl of laughter was a bitter sound. "That'll be the day."

"You thought you had your scam all figured out, didn't you, little lady?" He pulled her tighter against him, gave her a hard shake that she ignored.

"I'm close, but still working out the details."

"Well…" He relaxed his grip, pulled off

her dark shades and bumped the bill of her cap, knocking it to the ground. A mass of dark curls sprung free, cascaded across her shoulders. "You might want to start with *not* wearing sunglasses inside and doing a better job of squashing that Medusa look into submission. You could also use a course in the art of persuasive deception."

THE YOUNG WOMAN turned in Guy's arms. A smile alight with adoration flashed across the face that was quite lovely and very much resembled Guy's. She placed the palm of her hand gently against his jaw, patted softly, then pinched his earlobe and hung on tight.

"I've been studying the master of persuasive deception since the day you replaced Kate's dead hamster with a new one and nobody but me ever knew the difference! It's just a matter of time till I can slip one over on you, big bro."

She punctuated each sentence with a smart tug of his ear. He pulled her into a tender embrace, then buried his face in her out-of-control curls, giving the top of her head a loud kiss.

Abby watched, transfixed by the scene before her. She was still covering her mouth where she'd stifled the need to scream during the physical battle, the likes of which she'd only ever witnessed on television. Now that the skirmish had ended and she was one hundred percent sure this shoplifting imposter was a sister, Abby felt her knees go weak with relief. Even as she relaxed she felt a pinprick of envy over the sweet moment of physical closeness between the two.

With a jolt, the message to her senses was clear. She wanted to hold Guy like that, twine her arms around his taut middle and have him press his face to her hair. She turned, took a step away from the ridiculous notion as well as the scene.

"Abby, wait!" He'd caught sight of her. "I thought you'd already left."

She hesitated, not wanting to intrude on the touching reunion. Not wanting to deal with the thumping in her chest, the tightness in her lungs. The shame in her heart.

His warm touch guided her to turn toward him. She reluctantly complied, his hand still gently resting on her shoulder as he made apologies.

"I'm so sorry. I didn't expect anybody to witness our family theatrics. Did we scare you?"

She nodded, too flustered for coherent words.

"Here, let me introduce you to this brat, my baby sister, Casey." He turned to his sister and pulled her beneath his other arm. "Warden, this is Abby Cramer."

Ocean-blue eyes so much like Guy's flashed interest at the introduction.

"Not *the* Abby Cramer that I've heard so much about?"

"One and the same," he admitted.

He squeezed Casey affectionately, but with enough force that the woman flinched. Though he sounded normal enough, Abby sensed he was using brother-sister code to manage the direction of the conversation.

So, he'd spoken to his sister about her, huh?

Casey slipped from beneath his grasp and offered a hand. "Guy has such nice things to say about your family. I look forward to meeting them during my stay."

"Your stay?"

"Didn't he tell you?" Casey looked from her brother to Abby and back at Guy again before she made her point. "I'm here to begin the quality evaluation of this store. Guy's taken his sweet time on this project and we're almost behind schedule."

Then she rocked what Abby had just discovered was becoming the solid foundation of her very small world.

"Dad sent me, big bro. He wants you packed and on your way home by the end of the week."

CHAPTER EIGHT

NOT FOR THE FIRST TIME in his life, Guy wanted to pinch a purple place on Casey's arm. She delighted in rattling his cage, so it was never a surprise when she showed up like this, unexpected, unannounced and if she kept running her mouth, unwanted.

But he had to admit the zinger his little sister tossed out invoked a reaction from Abby that did worlds for his recently lagging self-confidence. The light leaked out of her eyes and the corners of her smile wilted like a thirsty houseplant. Then it got better. Her lips took on that same pinched pucker that Dillon got right before he let loose with a wail of discontent.

She cared about him. Guy felt sure of it. And not just because he was handy around the house.

"So, you won't be able to help finish up all the projects you and Daddy have planned?"

Then again, maybe not.

He wasn't completely certain of anything anymore. Well, that wasn't exactly true. He knew there was something special about Abby, something he felt compelled to get to know better if she'd let him. If only there was just a small corner of her heart ready and waiting to accept a new man in her life.

Just in case, he wasn't going anywhere.

"Do not let the Warden's ravings worry you," he assured Abby. "Casey thinks she's in charge of everybody, runs a tight prison."

"The Warden and the Admiral must be cut from the same cloth," Abby observed.

"Well said." Guy hadn't made the comparison before but Abby was right. His sister had very similar qualities to Sarah Reagan. He turned to Casey. "Abby just likened you to her rather tyrannical mother and I have to say she's right on the mark. You, baby sister, definitely have a streak of dictator in you."

"Don't make me box your ears," his sister warned.

He made fists, assumed a fighter's stance and took a playful swipe. A veteran of self-defense training, she expertly ducked, blocked the halfhearted punch and then threw a serious jab to his ribs. He yelped and backed away to a safe distance, rubbing his side while he made his case.

"Listen, kiddo, I've got at least a few more weeks worth of work here before I'm ready to head out. The Galveston project is on track to start in a few months. That gives me plenty of time to finalize the work I want to do at the Reagans' home."

"But Dad said…"

Guy gave her his infamous, no-nonsense look. "I'll handle everything. I always do."

"Yeah, right, just like you handled that debacle in Nashville."

The moment the criticism was out she bit her lip, censuring herself. Even for Casey, that was too far.

But it was hardly a secret. H&H had been under siege after a personal-injury lawsuit in their largest Tennessee location. The case was a matter of public record, but among the family all had privately been forgiven, if not forgotten. An extremely costly lesson learned, they'd moved on. But Casey just couldn't resist the occasional opportunity to scratch open Guy's still-fresh professional wound.

She stepped close and slipped her arm around his waist. "Sorry about that. The timing and the comment were insensitive."

"Just like you," he teased, letting her off the hook, knowing she was unlikely to do the same if the tables were turned. He glazed over the awkward situation by moving her an arm's length away so he could survey the shoplifter's disguise.

"That's quite a getup you've got there. I have to admit it's such a departure from your usual navy-and-white uniform that I hardly recognized you at first."

"Excuse me," Abby interrupted, "I have to be going."

Guy checked his watch. "Oh, of course. I'm sorry to hold you up. It is getting late."

"Late?" Casey glanced at the afternoon sun still high overhead.

"Well, yeah!" He admonished the sister who had no concept of time beyond her own workaholic schedule. "At five o'clock, when you have a baby to pick up from day care and someone at home expecting dinner and a ride to the hospital, it's getting late."

"Excuuuuuuse me." She flinched at his criticism, then quickly recovered, the look in her eyes telegraphing suspicion over his protective defense of any woman other than a member of the gaggle. No doubt, Casey would circle back around to that subject first chance she got. She scooped her cap off the sidewalk and tugged it over her curls.

"I'll wait inside so we can continue this conversation." Seemed the chance was hovering closer than even he expected.

"Abby," Casey said, turning her attention elsewhere. "It was a pleasure. I look forward to meeting the rest of your family soon."

"Thanks, but I don't know when that would happen."

"If there are home-improvement projects to be done, I'm an able volunteer. And at the very least you'll join us for the employee-appreciation barbecue. We have some great surprises planned for our employees."

"How do you know about all that?" Guy quirked a brow in question.

"There's not much in your life I don't know

about. Or won't eventually figure out." She smirked, touched the brim of her Dallas Cowboys cap in salute and breezed into the store.

"So that's what a female member of the Hardy clan is like?" Abby smiled and shook her head, her first taste of Casey being a typically spicy one.

"And she's the baby of the family. Aggressive but she's not even the bossy one. Wait till you meet Andrea."

"Will she be visiting, too?"

"Actually, no. I guess I was just thinking out loud." Or was it wishing out loud? If he showed up at home with a woman, his mother would faint. His sisters would never let him hear the end of it and his dad would start planning retirement, hoping his son was finally ready to settle down and take the helm.

There was no doubt about it. Guy was going to have to play twenty questions with Casey as soon as he went inside. In the past he'd always managed to come up with rather vague answers about his female friends that had appeased her. So why was it he actually wanted to share a few details this time? Maybe even rub in the fact that somebody might want him as a regular guy and not Guy Hardy, only *male* heir to the Hearth and Home empire.

Abby stirred beside him, needing to be on her way.

"Let me walk you to the car."

"Sure, if you don't mind." She ducked her head, but not quick enough to hide the small smile he hoped was evidence she wanted him near for a few moments longer. The simple acts of courtesy he'd been raised to provide automatically seemed to please her so much. Abby was possibly the most unspoiled woman he'd ever met. He waited while she unlocked the door of the compact car that hadn't seen the wet side of a soapy sponge in months and then he leaned in and opened it for her.

"Is it still okay for me to give Shorty a ride to the rehab center tonight?"

Abby slid into the seat, buckled herself with a snug tug of the belt and tilted her face toward him, squinting into the fading sun. "Why are you being so good to us, Guy?"

She was blunt. She deserved a straight answer, so he crafted one as best he could.

"Because I like you. All of you."

"And we like you, too."

She pinched her bottom lip between even, white teeth and sucked in a deep breath. Something important was coming. He squatted, hips to heels, so she was comfortably looking down into his eyes.

"We like you a lot. But your sister just reminded me that when you leave in a few weeks it'll just be me, Dillon and my folks again. You've gotta realize they might have some false expectations, Guy. You've been so kind to us that my family just naturally lights up when you're around. And that includes…"

She paused, swallowed, a furrow of distress settled between her lovely eyes. Was she about to say that included her?

"…That includes my son." She offered a sad smile. "Dillon's just a baby. He doesn't understand. He waits by the door and asks for you on the days you don't come by."

"Does that mean you'd like me to come by *every* day?" He was a high-school sophomore again, using his best bashful, hopeful smile to charm a pretty girl. He hadn't needed to change his approach in the twenty-some-odd years since he'd discovered that tactic worked like a charm. But the downward tilt at the outside corners of Abby's eyes told him it was going to be harder than that.

"You know what I mean." She touched his arm with her fingertips.

The rush of pleasure he'd felt was doused by a wave of remorse. The admission had been hard for her. She was trying to create something that would remind her son of his father, and another man's presence seemed to be working contrary to that effort.

He closed a hand over hers. "Yes, I do, and I promise I'll be very aware of your concern."

She began to pull away, to turn toward the business of starting her car. He increased the pressure on her hand. Her gaze met his, her eyes questioning.

"Abby, I truly care about your family, especially Dillon." *But you most of all.* "And you...well, you're an amazing young woman caught between a rock and a hard place, stuck in the middle, taking care of two generations. But you don't treat it as a burden. You see the pressures of your family's needs as blessings, and I find that remarkable. Mostly because I feel the same way about mine and I never thought I'd meet somebody outside of the Hardy clan who would understand."

She nodded. Words of confirmation were unnecessary. Despite their differences, this was common ground. Family was everything.

Even though he'd never take a wife, never have children of his own.

As he watched her car disappear from sight he took his time in the parking lot, gathering up shopping carts abandoned by customers.

Upstairs in the office, Casey had settled into his chair where she was studying the drawings on his desk.

"I have to admit I didn't see that one coming, even though Andrea mentioned you talk about this girl way too much for it to be anything as cut and dried as business."

"Andrea needs to keep her opinions to herself." He reached to roll up the plans.

Casey swatted his hands away and straightened the cheap reading glasses she'd fished off his desk so she could study the pages spread atop the cluttered surface. The oversize, drugstore horn-rims made her look like a barn owl. Add the thick, kinky mop topping off the disguise and his little sis was a real looker at the moment.

"Hmm…so these are the alterations you expect to make on the Reagans' home? Smart stuff, bro." She nodded approval as she continued to scan the draft. "And since all the changes are related to disability access we should be able to take this expense as a charitable deduction *and* get some great press from it. But I'm sure that's what you had in mind when you came up with this plan."

"Actually, this effort is absolutely not to be used for PR because it would embarrass the Reagans. And I don't intend to charge any of this against the company. I'll cover the cost myself."

Her head popped up.

"So Andrea's right. You've let this get personal."

"It's personal because these are nice people who deserve a break."

She yanked off the glasses and leveled the Hardy family eyes at him. The blue intensity never failed to bore into his very soul.

"Listen, I apologize for shooting my mouth

off in front of an outsider before, but you know I've got to say this now."

He lowered his chin and heaved a sigh. Yes, he knew quite well what was coming.

"Ike and Sadie Grossman seemed like that at first, too. But they were nothing but opportunistic trailer trash and, thanks to us they own every mobile-home park on the west side of Nashville today."

"You've just met Abby for yourself," he interrupted. "Her parents are good folks."

"Is that what the report confirmed?"

Guy hated to deceive anybody, but not being straightforward with family was an unpardonable sin. How could he get around this question without being dishonest with his sister, and right to her face? To make matters more pressing, whatever he said to the Warden now would most certainly be relayed to the rest of the family. He opened a file drawer as if he intended to produce a folder. He tried to be nonchalant with his carefully chosen words.

"The report's not final yet but the preliminary information is all positive."

"Not final? Are you using the same service? They've always been very efficient."

"The service is fine, just give them some time to do the work we pay them for. And speaking of that," he said, carefully tending a seed. "The company pays you way too much to have this kind of idle time on your hands, so I'd like you to get involved with the legals on the Galveston project."

She was silent. He glanced up to see her glowering at him, her arms crossed in defiance.

"What?" he demanded.

"That's always been your responsibility. Why are you trying to push something that important off on me?"

"Just trying to expose you to new details, but if you're not up to it…"

She lowered her chin and held a palm outward. "Stop right there. I know when I'm being baited so let's just save the games for one of your less discerning siblings." She glanced up, satisfaction gleaming in her eyes. "And as long as I'm doing my job *and* yours, how about if I make some phone calls to check up on the investigation?"

"Leave it alone, Casey." He averted his face, kept his hand occupied with the files. "I'm coordinating this one myself and if I need your help, which I won't, I'll ask for it."

Casey stood, crossed the few feet that separated them and pinched the fine hairs on his forearm, a tactic the gaggle found very effective in getting the undivided attention of their men. She gripped tightly forcing him to abandon his busy work.

"Alexander Theodore Guy! Tell me you're not smitten with that girl!" She tugged hard, demanding a response.

"Ouch!" He yelped and pulled Casey close to reduce the resistance. "And what would be so awful about that?"

"You cannot be serious! For starters, she's what? Twenty-five? Twenty-six? Way too young for a man looking down the shotgun barrel at forty."

Actually Abby was only twenty-four, so there was no defense there.

"Number two, if everything I've heard about her is on the up and up, the poor girl has got her hands full. She doesn't need a man who freely admits the time it takes to frame and dry in a new store is the perfect lifespan of a romantic relationship."

That was a ninety-day job so Casey wasn't far off the mark with her accusation.

"Three, she comes with a ready-made family, exactly what you've insisted your entire life that you don't want."

"You ladies change your minds at the drop of a hat. Why can't a man?" The question was just for argument's sake with Casey, but he was beginning to ponder that one for real.

She ended the painful tug-of-war and rested fists on her hips, double-huff style.

"Women may occasionally change their minds, but leopards don't ever change their spots. Bro, you have been adamant since you were fourteen that there's no wife and kids in your future and everything you've done since then has affirmed that assertion."

Casey's ability to cut straight to the bone was accurate, as always. What on earth had he been thinking? It was time to get back to business and bury these crazy daydreams that surfaced each time Abby was near.

His sister cupped his face in her cool hands and pulled him down close. "Now hear this, handsome stranger, I don't know what you've done with my brother, but hand him over! We have deadlines to meet and there's a fancy pair of boots in some Western-wear store in Galveston just waiting to become part of the Guy Hardy collection."

The drive from the little house a few blocks off Guadalupe to the rehab center seemed to take forever. Shorty had a hundred questions about the construction plan. Actually they were more objections than questions, a communication style Guy was becoming accustomed to hearing.

"I don't see how you can add another six square feet of floor space to the bathroom unless we blow out that side wall far enough to take down the neighbor's fence." The old fella was as antsy and short on patience as a kid on the last day of school.

"It'll work, Shorty. I've done the math." Guy tapped the roll of blueprints on the consol between them. "But don't take my word for it, you've got the drawings right there to prove it."

Shorty grunted, looked out the window.

"There can't possibly be a whirlpool tub that will fit into that space in the corner," he grumbled. "Not one we can afford anyway."

"One of our suppliers is bound to come up with just what we need."

"We'll never round up all the materials to finish this thing before Mother's Day."

"Of course we will." Guy was struggling with the negative comments. All he wanted to do was lock his thoughts on something positive. Something uplifting.

Something Abby.

"Are you as crazy about my girl as she seems to be about you or is it just the high pollen count that's got both your heads in a fog?" Shorty's voice was sour, as if he'd just taken a sip of dill pickle juice. The question sliced through the mental haze he had succinctly identified. Guy snapped to attention, considered the comment and the fact that the man beside him was, after all, the father of the woman he'd been daydreaming about and the man expected a straight-up response.

Guy risked a glance to his right. Incredibly, Shorty was grinning and scratching the new stubble of white whiskers on his chin.

"Well, Hopalong Cassidy, you gonna answer me or pretend you don't follow?" Eyes glinted beneath the bushy brows.

The truth of Abby's earlier statement cut deep. The gleam in her father's eyes said he hoped there might be something going on between his daughter and Guy. As much as he liked to make everybody happy, there was no point in leading the poor fellow on.

I don't want to hurt the Reagans or let my family down, but playing both ends against the middle has got me wondering which side I'm on anymore.

"I follow."

"And..." Shorty waited.

"And I think you're reading too much into my friendship with Abby."

"Friendship, huh?" He rubbed gnarled hands together and glanced out the passenger's window. "Friendship was what she had with Phillip, no matter how she tries to remember it for that poor dead boy's sake." Shorty dropped his chin and wagged his head side to side, then cut eyes at Guy that were dark pools of wisdom.

"No, sir, I see the way my girl stares at you

when you're not watchin'. And I don't believe I like it even one little bit. The last thing she needs is another man who values duty over his wife and child."

Guy pulled into the restricted parking zone and cut the engine. "Sir, the truth is I'd like to get to know Abby better in the few weeks I have left in Austin, and I hope we'll remain good friends after I leave. But she asked me just today to clear up misunderstandings that might lead to hurt feelings for anybody in your family. So I want to make my intentions on that subject clear before it's too late. Abby and I are friends, nothing more."

"Son, if that's really what you believe, it's already too late. There will definitely be some hurtin' later on. But I'm afraid you'll be the one doin' it."

PERCHED ON A TALL STOOL at the kitchen counter, Abby had a clear view of the H&H truck as it passed the front window and turned into her driveway. The men shouldn't be back for another couple of hours. Something had to be wrong. She abandoned her lesson plans and hurried toward the sharp knocking. Without checking the peephole, she yanked the door wide. As expected, there was a Hardy on her porch.

But it was Casey, not Guy.

CHAPTER NINE

"SO, WHERE'S THAT adorable baby boy of yours?"

Casey chirped the question as if arriving unannounced and uninvited on a virtual stranger's doorstep was the most normal thing in the world. She'd changed out of the overalls into tailored navy slacks with a white silk blouse. She wore a stunning pair of snakeskin pumps that Abby guessed cost more than her entire school teaching wardrobe. Did the whole Hardy family have a thing about expensive shoes and only wearing sneakers at home?

"What a nice surprise," Abby tried to sound pleased. She had a ton of work to get done, but she stepped aside and extended a hand inviting her guest in. "But if you're looking for Guy, I'm afraid it'll be a while before he and my dad get back." She returned to the kitchen with Casey following close behind.

"So, let me get this straight. Guy took off with your father for the evening and left you here alone?"

"Sure. He's been a huge help, offering to drive Dad to see my mom several nights a week. I run over there at lunchtime and then Guy takes Dad to visit in the evening."

"Whew!" Casey fanned the back of her hand across her forehead, pretending to wipe sweat from her brow. "For a while there I thought he was coming over here to see *you*. That would have been a disaster in the making."

The blunt words stung Abby like the unexpected attack of an angry yellow jacket. She assumed the composure she'd developed for dealing with the difficult parents of her schoolchildren.

"Casey, where would you get such a silly idea?"

"Yeah, it was dumb, wasn't it?" She chuckled and shook her head at what seemed to be an absurd thought. "But with that man, trust me, it's an easy mistake to make. I guess I didn't need to interrogate him so hard after all."

Interrogate him? No wonder he called this sister the Warden!

"Please don't be hard on your brother, and certainly not on my account. Guy's been very kind and a huge help to me."

"That's our boy all right." Her tone was a curious mixture of sarcasm and fondness. "He has this all-consuming savior complex, which explains why there's been a constant stream of women through his life. It's always been Guy to the rescue! The helpful hardware man making things right. He's bailed so many females out of their problems that it's second nature to him now. It's what makes him happy."

So there it was. Saving the day was how he got his kicks. It wasn't personal at all; it was his addiction. Casey was looking at her, waiting for a response. Abby's tongue went dry, like she'd just inhaled a mouthful of dust.

"Well, he seems like a wonderful man so I'm not surprised he's had his share of relationships." She forced the comment to sound casual when the truth was her ribs ached from the verbal sucker punch. Then things got worse.

"Relationships? Ha!" Casey threw her head back, whooped over what was obviously some inside joke. "That man has the attention span of a gnat when it comes to relationships. And no matter what he puts the ladies through, they give him the benefit of the doubt. I don't know what he says to charm them, but women always overlook his faults. At first, anyway."

"Faults?"

Casey arched one perfectly plucked eyebrow in that same skeptical way Guy did when Dillon offered up a bite of soggy cookie.

"Are you kidding? He relocates every nine months, works seven days a week, openly admits he has no intention of marrying, absolutely refuses to bring a woman home to meet our family and works on his art projects at crazy hours of the night.

"After a few months they get fed up with him, but sooner or later the poor fools show back up on his doorstep willing to compromise in case he's changed his mind about marriage." She stopped to swipe fingertips against the corners of her eyes where tears of hilarity gleamed. Then she let out a relieved sigh. "Honestly, Abby, I just had to come see for myself that you weren't one more in a long string of hopefuls."

Abby held both palms out, as if blocking the very idea. "Rest assured there's no chance of that. The two men in my life have my heart all filled up and there's no time for romance even if I was ready for it."

"Good, because even though he does it unconsciously at this point, Guy has turned pleasing females into an art form. And I'll be the first to admit it's the gaggle's fault. We're his training ground. He honed his charms with us and he is nothing if not subtle." She reached up and touched the small piece of colored glass suspended from the ceiling fan. "See, he's already left his mark on you, and my guess is this isn't the only piece of his work in your house." She gave the chain a pull and the blades overhead began a slow turn. "Is it?" Casey's eyebrows rose as she waited for a response.

Abby shook her head, remembering the comforting glow of the night-light in Dillon's room, the stained-glass sun catcher that had materialized in the window of the family area and the charming robin redbreast that hung from a suction cup in her laundry room.

She didn't even want to think about the lovely amethyst-filled geode that had appeared on her night table.

"Guy was always a silent shadow in the corner of the room, sitting so still we'd forget he was there. He listened to us talk about men, picked up all the right things we wanted to see and hear. And today he's an expert with women. Ever the champion fisherman. He sets the hook and settles back. He lets the catch run out of line, struggle with the circumstances and inevitably give up. Then he cuts and releases. And it's not the trophy he's setting free either. Oh, no, it's Guy Hardy who's getting off the hook."

Abby tilted her head, studied this woman who was full of information on the man who'd inserted himself into their lives and seemed determined to take charge in so many ways.

"Oh I love him," Casey continued, "but he's completely self-absorbed and for all of his thirty-eight years he's been adamant about never having a family of his own. I used to think that was all talk but the older he gets the more I believe he's made the right choice. Guy is not cut out to be a one-woman man and the Hardy women accept full responsibility for that."

Abby smiled to cover the confusion and the hairline fracture that split her spirit. No sophisticated X-ray technology could detect it, but the damage was done. She knew the pain of deep loss firsthand and suddenly sensed the potential for more looming in her future. So, there was a long string of this in his past, huh? It was easy to believe. Guy exuded an unusual charm. Oh, he was handsome in his snug jeans and fancy boots but his looks weren't the main attraction at all. He was educated and smart but in a practical sense so it wasn't like he threw off executive vibes that drew the power groupies.

The money might be an important element to certain women. It seemed he had plenty of that to meet all his needs and then some, but Abby had never been around wealth and had no expectations of doing so in the future. That definitely wasn't the draw. Not for her, anyway.

No, there was something special about Guy

that she hadn't been able to identify. And now it came to her.

He was… He was…

Endearing.

A quality that a number of women before her had evidently seen, admired, and tried to claim but failed miserably. And sooner or later they'd all wanted to come home, hoping he'd changed his mind about marriage. Was that how Casey had put it? Abby wanted to barf. She was on her way to being one more on the stringer after all.

Well, wake up girlfriend. Not anymore. You have a son to raise and parents who need you.

She ached inside but had to admit it was entirely self-inflicted. Guy hadn't made any inappropriate overtures, not even the slightest hint now that she thought about it. If anything, he'd probably treated her as another sister.

Ick.

And like an idiot she'd been the one to caution him against giving anybody the impression there was more than friendship between them? And here she was letting herself wax otherwise. Definitely time for a reality check.

And at that thought, Dillon howled.

"Oh, can I see him, please? If he looks anything like he sounds, he's a bruiser."

The interest in Casey's eyes was sincere.

"As long as you're not grossed out by a stinky diaper, I don't know why not." There was nothing to do but accept what she'd just learned and move on. Sadly Abby was adept in that area.

In Dillon's doorway she paused to give her son a chance to notice the newcomer. Standing in his crib, chubby fingers gripping the side rail, he stopped mid-wail. As usual there were no tears, just noise enough to call the cows home and produce a face the color of a boiled crayfish. Pleased with the results of his efforts, Dillon's pink lips curved and he ducked his head playing his "shy baby" game.

"May I?" Casey was considerate to ask permission. "I've just gotta cuddle him."

"Oh sure. He'll go right to you. The stinker can't resist a pretty woman who needs a hug."

Casey grinned. "Just like Guy!"

Something was up. Guy felt it the minute he helped Shorty into the house. Abby said the usual things, welcomed her dad home, asked after her mother, thanked Guy for his help, but there was a change in her. All business, no warmth. Not toward him anyway. Strangely, that was consistent with Shorty's behavior since he'd come rolling out of his wife's room.

Guy had lots of experience in the area of getting women past that claiming-nothing's-wrong pouting period into the here's-what-I'm-really-upset-about phase.

Shorty was a different story altogether.

He'd grumbled good-night and wheeled his chair down the darkened passage past Dillon's door where all was quiet.

"I'll be there to check on you in a few minutes," she called.

"Don't bother. Nobody wants to give me credit for it, but I can still pull my pants off and drag myself into the bed under my own steam," he snapped, obviously in a funk and spoiling for a fight.

"Daddy, wait."

Abby quirked a brow toward Guy in question before she abandoned the pile of papers she was sorting at the kitchen counter and made a beeline for her father. As she passed the light switch, she brushed her hand over the toggle, sending a slash of warm yellow light across the scarred wooden floor, illuminating the hallway. Shorty stopped his forward motion, sat with his back to them. Abby trailed her hand across his shoulders, crossed in front of him and squatted so she could look up into his eyes.

"What's wrong? Is it Mama?" she questioned, her voice soft.

Shorty glanced over his shoulder, acknowledging Guy was still present. They needed privacy.

"I'll see myself out," he offered.

"Wait for me on the back deck. I'll be there in a few minutes."

It was a statement, not a question. She hadn't even said *please*. He was obviously expected to comply. This was new territory with Abby. Yep, something was definitely up.

The full moon hung high above the tall Texas pines and cast a circle of light over the small backyard that smelled of treated lumber and honeysuckle vines. Guy's boots

clunked across the solid deck laid under
Shorty's watchful eye as he'd sipped coffee
and rattled off instructions between nonstop
stories of life back in the day. Before MS.
The poor man was at the end of his patience
with longing for his wife and there were still
a couple more weeks to go before she transi-
tioned home. Why else would he have imagined something was brewing between Guy
and Abby?

But Casey had made the same assumption,
with some help from big mouth Andrea. And
when they'd spoken on the phone two nights
ago even Meg, the oldest and most hands-off
sister, had quizzed him about what was holding him up in Austin. There was certainly a
common theme here, but was there a message? Great-Grandpa Hardy always said if it
brayed like a mule and kicked like a mule, it
must be a mule.

And would it be so bad if they were all
correct?

Would it be wrong if he and Abby did feel
an attraction?

There hadn't been anybody special in his
life in months, so maybe that was all there

was to it. Guy needed to find some quiet time to be still and listen to his heart for guidance. So far Guy hadn't found the right woman, but he was open to the idea of a relationship, just not a long-term one. And certainly not a permanent one that involved a family.

Some work with his hands would help. He needed to immerse himself in a glass project. Give himself time to think while he worked, sketching, soldering and creating meaningful beauty from jagged pieces of broken glass. It was his hobby that had gotten Guy through the debacle in Nashville and it would get him through this, too. Trouble was that for the first time he wasn't one hundred percent certain what he wanted the outcome to be.

"Guy." Abby's voice preceded the thwack of the screen door closing behind her. She moved into the warm glow of the outdoor lights he'd installed. Her face was serious, no hint of a smile or other indication she was happy to see him.

"We need to talk."

Oh great. That really meant she had something to say and he needed to listen up. Those words never boded well for the male on the receiving end of the "talk."

"So, what's up?"

She crossed to the wooden picnic table, raised a dollar-store flip-flop to the edge of the bench seat and stepped up to sit on the tabletop. She motioned for him to join her. She was comfortably dressed in what she'd once pointed out were her favorite pair of cutoff jean shorts, creatively patched with a rainbow bull's-eye on the tush. She also wore a T-shirt covered in small colorful handprints, a child's classic summer-camp art project. He couldn't help admiring the shapely thighs and muscles in her calves as he crossed the deck and took a seat on the bench opposite the end where she rested her feet.

"I'll park my ancient bones down here." He tried to keep things light, knowing that was probably a waste of time. When she didn't acknowledge his effort at age-difference humor, he got to the serious stuff. "Is something troubling Shorty?"

She slid a folded sheet of white paper from her hip pocket. "The social worker in charge of Mama's case at the rehab center came to see her today and he brought her this." Abby unfolded the paper and held it out for Guy.

He felt his eyes widen. It was a statement from the hospital.

For a *lot* of money.

"This is the portion of the bill that won't be covered by your insurance."

"Then that's the part I'll pay." Guy reached for the paper.

"You?" she quizzed, pulling the page to her chest. "Personally?"

"If necessary." He waited, but she still didn't hand over the itemized statement.

"Guy, it's one thing for insurance to cover expenses, and it's another entirely for you to give my parents a handout. I can tell you right now they won't accept anything they're not entitled to. Besides, they're accustomed to juggling medical bills."

"But that one doesn't need to add to their worries."

She shook her head, a sad realization curving her enticing rose petal pink mouth.

"When there's no hope of paying off the ones you have, one more really won't matter.

Like our lawyer says, 'You can't wring blood out of a turnip.'"

The words caught him off guard. Echoed, bouncing around in his mind. So similar to the statement he'd heard from their own corporate attorneys once the arbitration proceedings with the Grossmans had concluded.

So, the Reagans had sought legal counsel after all. Guy's heart dropped. Had he been wrong to trust them? This family was honorable, he was certain of it. But Abby herself had just admitted they'd spoken with a lawyer. If he'd used the investigation service, he might have discovered that sooner. Wouldn't Casey have a field day with that piece of information when she found out? And it was always a matter of when, never if.

He had to put this right in a hurry. Prevent this situation from spiraling out of control. He couldn't lose again, let the family down. He had to do something to protect his folks.

And he'd do just about anything for Abby if it would put a smile back on her lips.

Lips he was now certain he wanted to kiss.

CHAPTER TEN

"You might as well hand that over to save me some effort and grief when I contact our insurance company in the morning."

She stared at the page, seemed unsure what to do. The worry on her adorable face caused him to shrink inside. A clamp closed around his heart, squeezed it painfully.

"You're wasting your time, Guy. I've spent countless hours on the phone chasing down stuff like this for my folks just to recover a few double-billed dollars. It's like dealing with the IRS. You haven't done anything wrong and you give it your best shot but you know the odds are against you. That person on the other end of the line holds all the power and you're nothing but a faceless interruption to their day. You feel helpless and pathetic."

"Hon, it's a shame that at your young age you already have so much negative experience in that area." He kept his voice low and soft, appealing to her as he would a frightened child. Which is exactly what she looked like at the moment. "But I'm in a much different position. Remember, Hearth and Home is the insured party and I have the ability to cancel a significant contract with this provider if I'm not satisfied with the outcome of this settlement. So how about letting me throw my executive weight around and see if I can get them to reevaluate these expenses that don't appear to be covered?"

He extended his hand, took the edge of the paper between thumb and forefinger and tugged.

She held tight.

"Please, Abby? You don't have to fight this one alone."

Her fingers relaxed but the set of her jaw told him reluctance was still holding her hostage. He slid the page gently from her grasp. She resisted for a moment then let it slip free. Without another glance at the offending document, he folded it and stood to tuck it into his hip pocket.

Her head hung, she stared at empty hands.

What was she thinking? He stepped in front of where she sat, touched two fingers beneath her chin and tilted her head upward. The overhead lights cast shadows from her wayward curls across her face. It was difficult to tell whether the gleam in her eyes was from the threat of tears or surprise at his gentle touch.

He was a grown man, experienced in every way, but in an instant he was that high-school sophomore again. He'd never longed to kiss a woman so much in his life and had no idea how to address the feeling.

The timing was completely wrong. If she was offended, he'd blow what might be his only chance to show her his heart. If she kissed him back, he'd never know if it was because she returned his feelings of if it was just gratitude. The last thing he wanted was attention from another woman just because he'd bailed her out of a jam. He'd had enough of that in his life.

No, this was infinitely different. There was an unfamiliar tingling in his chest. His knees felt unsteady, wobbly. But it was a good wobbly, replete with chills that were out of place on this warm Texas night.

The gleam in her eyes intensified. Shadows didn't hide the fat tear that leaked from the corner of her left eye, trailed down her cheek and clung to her stubborn jaw.

He slid his hand upward, tenderly smoothed away the tear then took the liberty of sinking his fingers into her silky curls. He leaned from the waist, ducked his head and, though he was nearly desperate to touch his lips to hers, instead he placed a chaste kiss on the crown of her head.

ABBY WANTED TO shrivel up and die right there on top of her cedar picnic table. She'd been so sure he was about to kiss her she'd almost closed her eyes and puckered up. Thankfully she'd been too chicken to do that or she'd really seem like a lovestruck kid right now.

He'd kissed her all right. On the head! Just the way he'd done with Casey.

Guy really does think of me like another sister! How disgusted he would be if he knew the reason I'm sitting on this table is that I want to hug him so badly I can't trust my

*knees to hold me up. I need to stand on my
own as I always have and not rely on Guy
like so many women before me.*

She tensed at the thought of making a nit-
wit of herself before a man who'd been nothing but good to her family. A man who was
honorable, mature and accomplished in so
many facets of life. Every muscle in her body
tightened with anxiety over what he must be
thinking of her weakness. Of her tears of self-
pity! How embarrassing!

Guy must have felt the shift in her body
language. His hands slowly dropped to his
sides. He took a careful step back. His motions were cautious, like he was dealing with
a potentially explosive situation. Was that
how he thought of her? A ticking time bomb
that had to be handled with care? Another
sister who needed the kid-glove approach?

She had to put a stop to the useless fantasies that had somehow crept into the few
quiet spaces in her mind. All evidence confirmed it. Guy didn't even remotely see her as
a romantic interest. How stupid she'd been to
warn him that her folks thought there might
be something brewing between the two of

them. He must have gotten a belly laugh over that one.

She surreptitiously swiped at another run-away droplet as she shoved a hand through her hair. She didn't believe for a moment that her motions fooled him, but at least she was trying to maintain a shred of dignity. His sisters sounded like strong women. There was nothing strong about her right now, not when all she wanted was to curl into a tight ball and dissolve in a puddle of self-pity. Hopefully this paltry effort at composure would earn her a little respect.

Respect. Lots of people found love but respect was often harder to come by. Yes, she'd settle for that if it were all she could have. Not the stuff fantasies are made of but she didn't have time for daydreams anyway.

"Whew!" she huffed. "I just about let the pressures of life with Sarah and Shorty Reagan get to me that time." She forced a smile, propped her elbows on her knees and met Guy's sympathetic gaze straight on. "Sorry about that."

His brows drawn together, he studied her. She was glad for the new outdoor lights so she could see his handsome face, note the way he pressed his lips together whenever he was considering what to say.

"No apology necessary. My—"

"I know. I know." She held up a palm, dismissing what he was about to say and closed her eyes, resigned. "With five sisters somebody was probably blubbering all the time so you're used to it."

Guy's hand closed around hers and she absorbed his warmth, tingling as it shot from her fingers to her bare toes. Her gaze flew open, locked on his as he spoke.

"I was about to say my emotions would be at a fever pitch all the time if I had half the stressors on me that you carry around constantly. So don't apologize and don't hold back. If you need a shoulder I'm here for you, even if it's just to carry two-by-fours. Deal?" He switched from hand-holding to a hand-shake position.

"Deal."

They shook twice and she prepared to let go. He held on.

"And is it also a deal that you'll let me do

a full investigation of this hospital statement before you lose sleep over it?"

She was silent, not sure she had other options anyway.

"Abby?" His voice was hopeful, his blue eyes so kind. How could she not trust him with this situation when she was basically powerless to affect the outcome?

"Sure," she agreed, feeling a small wave of relief at giving this burden over to him. No wonder all the women in his past remained hopeful, waiting for him to have a soul-mate epiphany. That endearing quality was a powerful force that inexplicably drew them toward Guy like the moon pulled out the tide.

"Great." He released her, slapped his hands together and rubbed them, a look of accomplishment on his face as if he'd just closed a big contract.

There it was again. More evidence that she was business, not pleasure.

"Now, let's talk about a couple of areas where we do have some control," he continued. "First, what do you do for stress relief?"

It was a basic question but one that had no

answer he'd find acceptable. So she simply shrugged.

"Yep, just what I suspected. We're going to have to change that."

"And how about you?" She turned the tables, uncomfortable being the center of his concern.

"I have a hobby that lets me focus on something besides myself and corporate worries. It's creative and restorative and I feel a sense of accomplishment that comes from working with my hands."

"Really?" She waited for him to tell more, to claim the beautiful stained-glass pieces he'd anonymously positioned in her home.

"Yeah." A sense of creative pride glowed in his eyes. "But the point is that I have something to do that lets me get outside of my head for a few hours. It recharges me. Has there ever been anything in your life like that?"

"Of course." She didn't have to think that over at all. "Competing on the rodeo circuit always had that type of effect on me. Winning was nice but it wasn't everything. Just making a connection with the horse and running a clean cloverleaf pattern was so energizing. I couldn't wait to get to the stables after school. Even the days when I didn't ride, when all I did was muck out stalls and groom animals, I always came home happy." The memories were vivid; the sounds and smells were as real as if they were still part of her life. "Exhausted and smelly, but happy."

"Okay, then we need to find an outlet that will give you that same sense of exhilaration." He pinched his nose and continued in a nasal twang. "Maybe minus the smelly part."

They nodded agreement and smiled at the silliness.

"Okay, let's talk about another area where we have some control. How about if we take your family to the H&H barbecue next weekend? Your mom seems to be doing so well, I couldn't help but wonder if the doctor would give us a day pass so we could take her out for some fun."

"But that's just for your employees, isn't it?" Abby's family would never crash a store function. And the last thing she wanted to do was give anybody else the absurd impression there was anything more than friendship between herself and their boss.

"If you'll recall, my sister's already expecting you. Aside from that, half the store employees knew or have met your family in the past month. They'll be thrilled to see your mother up and around. It'll reward their efforts and prayers, so how about it?"

Guy was right, as usual. How awesome of him to be the one to suggest they take her mother out of the rehab center for a break. It would do wonders for her parents to spend a carefree day together and was probably just the interlude they needed to get them through the final weeks of separation.

Final weeks.

She glanced at her watch to confirm the date then calculated the remaining number of days. Abby's spirit plummeted at the thought of all the work that had yet to be accomplished on the playground. She felt a Dillon-size pout coming on.

"What?" Guy's voice was insistent. "You looked all enthusiastic and then your face fell like somebody stole the last corn dog at Curbo's."

She couldn't help but smile. He really did try hard in so many ways.

"I'm sorry, it's just that I only have a couple weekends left to get the project completed and I can't possibly give up next Saturday."

He huffed a sigh, and shook his head.

"Hon, I know you want to do everything yourself and I understand why. I even understand the reason you'd rather not have any help from me, though it doesn't make any practical sense at all. But there are plenty of other people who'd gladly pitch in with painting and planting. In fact—" he snapped his fingers then tapped his temple "—I've arrived at the perfect solution. I'm drafting Casey to be your right hand until the playground is finished."

"I can't take advantage of your sister. She's a professional woman with a lot of responsibilities of her own."

Guy put his hands on his hips, arched his back and hooted up at the stars. Abby marveled at the sight of his unrestrained laughter. He tried to talk at the same time but the merriment took his breath away and made it impossible to comprehend his words.

Though she didn't quite understand what was so funny, the hilarity was infectious.

Abby began to snicker and snort at his laughter, which only made Guy wrap his strong arms around his sides and laugh that much harder. Eventually he ran out of steam, leaned forward with his hands on his knees and labored to catch his breath.

"Now, will you explain what was so funny about me being considerate of your little sister?"

"Oh, the idea of sweet, unpretentious Abigail Cramer worrying about taking advantage of the Warden is just priceless. That woman is a professional busybody, a workaholic and barracuda. She's here three weeks early and she knows it. She can't stand not being all up in my business, trying to best me at every turn. The fact that this is something she can do that I can't will drive her to work as if her next meal depends on it. You are about to see Casey Hardy at her finest."

"Well, she did say she was an able volunteer if there were home-improvement projects to be done," Abby recalled.

He wore the broadest smile Abby had seen on him yet, and that was saying something because this man was basically a happy camper. She had to admit he seemed to lack for nothing, which helped explain why he was perfectly at peace with his life the way it was. No wonder he wasn't looking for any change.

"If you're sure." She still wanted to give him the chance to reconsider.

"Oh, I'm positive. You just plan to meet the two of us tomorrow after school and tell her what remains to be done and leave it to Casey to throw her heart and soul into the work."

"But there's still stuff I want to do myself." She was skeptical that take-charge Casey would take over.

"And she'll respect that. Remember, she's the youngest of six. She learned the hard way that when Meg and Tess told her to stay out of their closets there was a price to pay when she invaded their space. And it took Kate and Andrea locking her out of their bathroom for a week to teach Casey their makeup was off-limits. So she's schooled in the ways of re-specting another woman's territory. You just tell her where the line is and she'll toe it."

"But she doesn't seem to have that kind of respect for *your* boundaries." Probably a bit too direct, but then Casey had shown up on the doorstep a few hours earlier all too willing to spill the beans on her brother.

He stilled, quieted, his eyes narrowed with introspection. "Oh, she respects me all right. It's just we're the only two kids who inherited our dad's competitive spirit and we got it in spades. Neither of us is ever content to rest on our laurels. There's always a bigger prize to be had and she delights in trying to beat me to it."

"From what I've seen so far, she's quite a character. I think we'll get along just fine." Abby gave in, knowing she had to have help from somewhere. A strange flutter filled her chest as her heart wiggled like a child's wooden top, spinning and whirling out of control.

"That's exactly what I figured you'd say when I imagined you two meeting. I know you'll feel the same about all my sisters."

The look on his face was puzzling. Hope and happiness tinged with a strange touch of sadness glinted in his mesmerizing eyes. Eyes she would miss terribly one day.

Eyes Abby feared she'd begun to…

Love.

CHAPTER ELEVEN

THE PLAYGROUND parking lot was empty when Abby arrived except for the familiar H&H vehicle that had become a symbol of comfort. Even as she had the thought, she felt the ache of sorrow, knowing her remaining time with Guy was slipping away.

The passenger door of the truck flew open and Casey bounded to the ground leaving no further time for spirits to lag. The slender brunette was lean and athletic, the muscles in her arms defined by a life of physical activity. By contrast Abby felt short and dumpy, still carrying weight in her legs and backside that she'd gained during pregnancy. She tugged the hem of her shorts at a futile attempt to cover her thighs.

Guy hadn't exaggerated the thick mop of corkscrew curls that seemed to have a mind of their own, spiraling and waving in the warm wind. Though Casey must have been five years older, her energy level made Abby feel like a worn-out gym sock. An excited grin split Casey's face as the beauty loped across the asphalt.

The driver emerged from the white vehicle and Abby's insides lurched, then did a skip and a jump at the sight of Guy Hardy. He winked and raised his hands in surrender as if helpless to stop the speeding train that was his kid sister.

Abby was quickly engulfed in a friendly hug, her back being patted affectionately.

"Thanks so much for letting me help with your project!" Casey enthused. "I love working outdoors and I've always had the greenest thumb in the family. I guarantee Guy can kill plastic ivy so he's definitely not the right choice when it comes to gardening." This last was said loud enough for anyone in the parking lot to hear, definitely meant to goad her brother.

"I hate to admit it, but she's right," he gave in easily, as he reached Casey's side. "My forte is working with inanimate materials. The only green things I get along with are the ones in my salad bowl."

He rifled fingers through his sister's wild locks.

"Are you sure you don't want me to stick around? I'm really good with a brush and I see that jungle gym still needs another coat." He indicated the dome-shaped set of climbing bars that were only half-covered in rust-resistant paint. Tedious work she'd been avoiding.

Abby hesitated, loving the hopeful way his forehead was wrinkled in question. Then she caught sight of the young pecan tree, remembered her mission and shook her head. Maybe a little too emphatically, because the light in Guy's lovely blue eyes dimmed just a bit. His smile slipped slightly as he rocked back on the heels of his boots and shrugged. She'd been close to giving in, to accepting his offer of help just to make his day. And she could use the extra pair of capable hands.

"Oh, don't fall for that sad puppy look of his, Abby. Stick to your guns and send him packing. Besides, after the last swing set he put together he said he'd never get himself in that position again."

"Is that so?" Abby folded her arms and waited for the story that was sure to follow.

"Tell her, Guy. What was the name of that redhead you dated in Nashville? April? Amy?"

"I don't remember." He scowled at Casey.

"Oh sure you do. What was her name? Angel!" Casey snapped her fingers over finding the right answer. "That was it, Angel Merrett. You said she was the total package except for those two little monsters masquerading as children."

"I doubt I was that crude," he defended himself. "But those boys *were* out of control."

"Oh, tell Abby. It's hysterical!"

"I think I'd better get going." He began to back away, distancing himself from his sister and her tale.

Casey turned to Abby, chuckling as she recalled the story. "To be fair, nobody blamed him for feeling that way after we heard what happened." She leaned in. "He was helping her save a few bucks by delivering and assembling the new backyard stuff she bought at our store for her kids. Guy took his boots off so he wouldn't scuff the equipment while he attached the swings and slide. When he was distracted the little brats filled his boots with what they thought was mud!"

Abby sputtered laughter behind her hand. "Is that true? They put mud in your boots?"

Guy heaved a resigned sigh and turned back toward the two women. "Not just any boots, either. The first and only pair I've ever owned that were completely custom-made. They were beauts."

"Ask if he still has them." Casey gave Abby a conspiratorial wink.

Guy growled like an angry bear at his sister's insistence upon the details. Undeterred, she encouraged Abby again. "Go ahead, ask him what he did with that pair."

Abby took a step closer to Guy, daring to follow Casey's lead. "So, what became of the boots?"

"One of them is in my mom's laundry room and the other is in Meg's basement. They're used as doorstops."

"Huh?" Abby didn't quite follow the transition from fancy footwear to doorstop.

Casey couldn't resist beating him to the punch line.

"The 'mud' the boys put in Guy's boots

was really quick-dry concrete that he'd mixed up in the wheelbarrow to anchor the swing set into the ground!"

Guy grimaced. "By the time I caught on to their prank, the concrete had already set up. My boots weighed about eight pounds apiece."

Abby made no effort to hold back the cackle of laughter.

"Hence, my brother's handmade boots became the world's most stylish doorstops."

"Well, I don't know about most stylish but they certainly were the most pricey." He rolled his eyes skyward over the loss, while the ladies continued to share a hearty laugh at his expense. When it was clear they wouldn't give up the fit of giggles anytime soon, he turned toward the truck. "You girls enjoy yourselves. I'm glad I could provide a little comic relief for you today."

"Thank you!" Abby called amid the dwindling chuckles. Guy climbed inside the truck and with a wave out the window merged into the afternoon traffic.

"Ooohhhh, that man is so much fun to pester. Just another reason he's so popular with the ladies."

The reminder of his appeal with the women sobered Abby. Time to get to work. The one thing that took her mind off her worry. Good thing there was lots of work because there were lots of worries.

She clapped her hands once and rubbed them together. "Shall we get busy?"

"Absolutely!"

The time they spent together was further confirmation of Casey's high-spiritedness. No wonder she was a workaholic. The woman had the energy to burn brightly for eighteen hours a day with enough left over to power a small generator!

Her ideas were endless, too. While she seemed to honor the original dream for the playground, she threw out an innovative suggestion for a quiet meditation area adults could use when the kids were not around.

Aside from the mile-wide assertive streak that made her so competitive, Abby was beginning to think Casey was perfect, too. They'd warmed to each other quickly and Abby could tell Casey would be a loyal friend. Maybe this was what it was like to have a sister.

Hmmmmm… A sister. Was that just one more way Guy was trying to help her out? Was she intended to become an honorary member of the gaggle?

Hours later they rested on a concrete bench beneath the shady canopy of a spreading live oak tree, and recapped what remained to be accomplished. Casey checked items off her growing list, as she drew a time line on her pad and noted what had to be done before their Mother's Day dedication.

"Casey?"

"Hmmmmm?" Her head was lowered over her work, curls obscuring those intensely blue eyes.

Abby kept her voice casual, needing a few answers but not wanting to tip her hand too far.

"I can't tell you how much I appreciate your help. Do you pitch in like this for all of your brother's lady friends?"

The sable corkscrews bounced with the motion of Casey's head popping up, her eyes seeking Abby's.

"Oh, no! Guy hasn't introduced a woman to us since college. Isn't that amazing? He's always kept his romantic involvements away from the family to prevent anybody from getting the wrong idea about his intentions. He shares a funny story about one of them now and again, but only after they've moved on. So it caught all our interest when we heard 'Abby this and Abby that' over and over." She winked. "Obviously, there's a very special friendship between you two. We may have to declare you and Dillon honorary members of the Hardy clan so the whole family can get to know you."

Abby's temples pounded as blood rushed to her head. She hoped her face wouldn't flush and give away the pleasure she felt knowing this was something unique for Guy, just as it was for her. Of course Casey meant it innocently, had no idea Abby had pipe dreams of more. How would it feel to be loved by a big family?

But more importantly, how would it feel to be loved by Guy?

A breeze ruffled her bangs, trailing them across her eyes. She pushed them back from her face, glanced up, her gaze locking on the low white fence that surrounded the pecan sapling. It was young and vulnerable, just like Phillip had been when she'd known him as a boy.

Phillip. She hadn't thought of him in days.

Oh, how can I be so forgetful? My sweet Phillip has been gone such a short time and his memory is already slipping away from me. How can I be so infatuated with Guy that I can't keep my mind on the precious friend who loved me with his last breath?

A slender arm draped across her back. A soft hand cupped her shoulder and pulled her close.

"You okay, kiddo? I don't think you heard a word of what I just said."

She'd completely tuned out Casey's chatter, fixed on her private thoughts. "I'm sorry, what did you say?"

"I was telling you we should lay tiles instead of trying to pour a walkway. That would be much faster and free if we use discards from the H&H stockroom. We always put the seconds and mismatched tiles aside to be recycled but it's still high-quality material and there's no reason I can't donate it to the playground instead. What do you think?"

Abby needed to unburden, but this was Guy's sister and they were just getting to know one another.

"I have some stuff on my mind that I have to work through before I can make any more decisions today."

Again, there was a comforting squeeze, then Casey spoke.

"If you need to talk, I'm a good listener. I spent most of my childhood being a fly on the wall. You can't possibly say anything I haven't already heard at least once from one of my older sisters," she encouraged. "And even though you've probably experienced more of life's setbacks than I have, I do have a few years on you and can probably give you some sage feedback."

Instinct told Abby she could trust this woman.

"You know I'm building this playground as a tribute to my late husband, right?"

Casey nodded. "That's what Guy said."

"Well, it just occurred to me that I haven't thought of him for several days." Her chin drooped. She was ashamed to look Casey in the eye. "How can I be such a hypocrite? I'm trying to create a place to keep Dillon from forgetting the father he's never known, and I'm already losing touch with the memories of the boy who was my best friend for most of my life. I feel like such a failure."

"Oh, Abby, you're not a failure at all. Your heart is just mending."

Could it be that simple? "You think so?"

"Yes, I do. You've always heard time heals all wounds, right? The longing for what was lost may linger for a very long time, but we eventually get past the physical ache that makes us think we can't go on. I'd guess that since you can go a few days at a time now without thinking of…"

"Phillip."

"If you can go a couple of days without thinking of Phillip then your heart is on the mend. You might even be ready to consider letting somebody new into your life."

Abby straightened away from the kindly embrace. After their conversation the night before, she was determined not to give the impression that she was indeed another one of Guy's doomed hopefuls.

She shook her head. "I don't think that'll happen anytime soon, though you may be right about the healing. What I feel these days is more akin to guilt than sadness."

"Well, you haven't done anything to feel guilty for so don't bother with that emotion. It's a monumental waste of energy." Casey stood, brushed down the front of her khaki shorts and glanced at her wristwatch. "I know you need to get home soon and Guy will be back to pick me up any minute now. So, let's go over your plans one more time to make sure I understand what you want, then I'll be able to come back tomorrow and get started."

Abby stood and wrapped Casey in a brief hug. Though she was younger, shorter and broader than Guy's sister, Abby felt a strong kinship with Casey that had nothing to do with age, shape or size.

"I SHOULD HAVE MY HEAD examined for offering you my pullout sofa till you can find a place of your own."

The siblings sat across the rented dining-room table from one another that evening. The fragrance of green curry wafted from white containers as they heaped Thai food on paper plates.

Casey was in one of her probing moods and Guy found himself on the receiving end of her questions, as usual. He preferred solitude and quiet at the end of the day, some peace to concentrate on his art. Tonight there would be none of that. The roomy two-bedroom apartment H&H leased for him during his stint in each new city was shrinking by the moment. Casey was a fizzy drink that had been shaken too hard. Her effervescence filled a room to overflowing, gobs of popping bubbles in her wake. Yet again Guy feared for the poor schmuck who fell in love with his kid sister.

"If you'd put a bed in that second room instead of spreading your amazing array of toys out everyplace, I could just stay here with you."

"Those are artisan's tools, not toys," he reminded her for the umpteenth time. Just because she had no artistic skill of her own, she poked fun at his love for working with stained glass. The day he was stationary enough to blow glass, not just cut and solder it, she'd truly be amazed by what kind of "toys" would be required.

"And as much as you're welcome to visit, staying here is *not* an option, Rebecca Thelma Casey. After sharing a bathroom with you girls for all those years, I've earned my personal space. Besides I need all my equipment with me so I can finish the piece I'm doing for Mom."

He'd proudly shown Casey the colorful display of frosted yellow daffodils and gleaming orange tiger lilies. The four-foot-square pane of intricate glass would eventually replace a window in the family kitchen back home. It would be a radiant reminder of summertime when their mother sat at her breakfast nook during the freezing Iowa winters.

"I have to hand it to you, bro. You've definitely put the gaggle on notice that this Mother's Day your gift is the one to beat." She popped spicy calamari into her mouth.

He shook his head. "I have another project I have to do first. I'm shooting for Mom's birthday at the end of June. I'll be back home by then and I can install it myself. She's been after me for years to do this for her so I can't wait to see her face the first time she gets a look at it."

"Then you really are planning to go home in a couple more weeks?"

"Well, yeah. There's easily three months of planning at corporate before I have to move down to the Galveston site."

"And what about that sweet girl and her family?"

Guy's chopsticks stilled, spring roll halfway to his mouth. He narrowed his eyes, deciding whether to play dumb or come clean.

Maybe halfway was best.

"Sweet girl, huh? Considering you were full of suspicions yesterday, you sure have become a fan overnight."

"Trust me, I still want to see the final report on the Reagans, but if first impressions pan out I agree we don't have any long-term worries."

Several things assaulted Guy at once. The report the family was waiting on. He had to do something about that, and soon.

Then there was the conversation he'd had

with their insurance agent that morning. Don Quinn was the owner of the independent Iowa firm. He'd worked with H&H since the beginning and stuck with them even after the arbitration with the Grossmans that had cost a small fortune to settle. Don was adamant that the coverage provided on the Reagans case was far beyond fair and equitable. The injury had not been a result of negligence on the part of Hearth and Home. It was confirmed by the Reagans own surgeon to be a spontaneous fracture, not uncommon in a woman Sarah's age. Given the recent history of payout, Don stood firm in his refusal to offer a gratuitous settlement beyond what was contractually required.

Sarah still had months of physical therapy ahead of her that would not be covered. It would add up to tens of thousands of dollars Shorty could never pay. That could ultimately jeopardize their only significant asset, their home. Guy was prepared to cover it all out of his own pocket, but how could he do that without offending the Reagans? And if he told them the truth of his conversation with Don, would they take their case to their attorney after all? Even a claim that was doomed from the start could tie up the family for months in litigation and run up a huge tab for the lawyers involved. If that happened, the family sure enough would know he'd rolled the dice and gone outside of their agreed upon procedure that was designed specifically to protect H&H.

A procedure required because he'd messed up in Nashville.

And if all that wasn't enough, there was the matter of Shorty having turned surly again. Abby said mood swings were just part of day to day life with the multiple sclerosis, but this one seemed to be settling in for a while. Shorty had been grumpy and argumentative today, not wanting to work out the details of their reconstruction plans that should be well underway.

Guy checked his watch, wondered if Dillon was already down for the night. If he hurried...

"Don't you agree?" Casey tapped the edge of Guy's plate with her chopsticks.

"Huh?"

"What is it with people tuning me out

today?" she demanded, her face turned to the ceiling as if expecting a celestial response.

Guy smiled at her mock frustration. "Sorry. I'm listening now."

"I said for being so young Abby really has a great head on her shoulders. She's a darling girl. And by the way, she has one whopper of a crush on you that's stopped her from thinking about Dillon's father for days at a time."

"She told you that?" He held his breath.

"Not in so many words. Are you gonna eat that last bite of calamari?" Without waiting for a response, Casey speared the fried squid with the tip of her chopstick and raised it to her open mouth. As she munched, she continued, "And don't think for a minute, Alexander Theodore Guy, that I don't see the same look in your eyes. You've got a thing for that the cute little blonde and it has nothing to do with professional obligation. Admit it."

"You know me better than that." He ducked his head and busied himself with his meal. Maybe playing dumb would have been the best choice after all.

"Sooner or later, you'll talk." The Warden

nodded her head, certain her prisoner would eventually fess up.

"There's just nothing more to say on that subject, that's all."

"If you say so, bro." She winked. "How about pulling out the sofa and helping me make up the bed before you leave?"

"It's almost eight. What makes you think I'm going out again?" The woman had a sixth sense. Scary.

Under the table she tapped her bare foot against his ankle.

"You've still got your boots on, cowboy. My guess is you're going to drop by and see if there's anything you can do tonight to help out that little filly." She shook her head. "And I sure hope she turns you down. There needs to be at least one woman in the world who doesn't want Guy Hardy to come to her rescue."

Nope. Casey wouldn't let him off the hook. Ever.

But, please let her be wrong about Abby.

CHAPTER TWELVE

FROM HER COMFORTABLE position in the rocking chair, Abby heard truck wheels grind to a stop in the driveway, then the slamming of a heavy door. Dillon responded immediately, squirming in her lap where they'd been snuggled for ten minutes to quiet him for the night. She should be annoyed, since it was almost time to put her son down. Instead her heart shimmied in her chest at the thought of a visit from Guy.

She kept her seat, waited for the knock, didn't want to seem as if she'd been expecting him. But truth be told she'd been thinking of him since they'd said their goodbyes at the playground. At home, during their favorite dinner of tomato soup and grilled cheese, Dillon had pointed toward the front door and asked for Guy repeatedly. It was the same pitiful way he called for his Cookie Monster doll when it fell out of the crib at night.

Her spirit was torn and the wound worsened by the minute. Just as Phillip would never come home, Guy would never be hers. And she'd discovered *never* was a long, long time. He could only be a friend passing through her life, helping to smooth the way as much as she'd let him. That was all he was willing to give and she had to accept it just like the hopefuls who'd gone before her.

Besides, he didn't even think of her as more than another sister. How sick that she wanted him to do otherwise.

Knuckles wrapped softly. He was a considerate man.

"Guy!" Dillon shouted. He wiggled hard for his mama to release him. She rocked forward, settled him on his bare feet and watched the light of her life waddle across the old wooden floor. When he reached his destination, he slapped both palms hard against the surface and called with glee, "Guy!"

The single word from Dillon spoke volumes about the condition of his tiny heart.

A low rumble of laughter could be heard through the hollow core of the door. Abby released a sigh and knew the wonderful flutter of butterfly wings that always accompanied the sound of Guy's voice. She threw the dead bolt and opened her home to the only man who'd ever made her feel such things.

With the abandon only a child can display without embarrassment, Dillon launched his stout body against Guy's legs. Chubby arms wound tightly around shins and a small happy face burrowed into faded blue jeans.

"Guy!" he squealed. The delight was enough to lodge a lump the size of Dallas in Abby's throat. Her baby desperately needed a daddy and he mistakenly thought he'd found one.

Guy squatted and opened his arms to Dillon, who didn't hesitate. The two melted together, held each other tight and exchanged noisy raspberry kisses as if their forty-eight hours apart had been a lifetime of separation. Guy stood, hugged Dillon to his chest and locked eyes with Abby.

His were shiny, welled up with unshed tears.

The sight took her breath away. This incredible man loved her son.

Oh, if he could only care about me that way.

Guy cleared his throat, blinked hard and stole another noisy helping of neck sugar from the toddler who was completely content to be pressed against the broad chest.

"Hey, leave some for his mama," she teased to help all of them past the emotions of the moment.

"Are you kidding?" He jostled Dillon, getting shrieks of delight for his trouble. "This bruiser is one quarter nails, snails and puppy-dog tails and three quarters honey-puffs cereal. He has enough sweetness to last a lifetime."

"You're pretty sweet yourself, you know that, Mr. Hardy?" She smiled up into his incredible blue eyes, wondering if he had any inkling how her heart was tap dancing.

He shifted Dillon to the crook of one arm, opened the other and waited.

But not for long.

She stepped into the comfort of Guy's embrace, snaked her arm around his middle, pressed the side of her face to his chest and listened to the wild thumping inside. The three of them shared their first group hug and Abby committed the moment to treasured memory in case it never happened again.

She forced herself to ease the pressure she'd applied around his taut waist and tipped her head back, expecting to see pity in his eyes that her need for physical contact was as blatant as her son's. What he telegraphed with his gaze was far from pity.

Guy dipped his head and touched his lips to hers. Softly, with no insistence. Gently, making no demands.

"What is all that ruckus about at bedtime?" Her dad's voice carried down the hallway just before they heard the squeak of his chair.

She went to pull away but Guy held her to his side.

"It's okay. I can hug you two, can't I?"

"Sure," she agreed. There was nothing wrong with that between friends, was there? *But what about that kiss I was about to return?*

"Papa," Dillon greeted his grandpa but made no move to lean away from Guy's arm.

"Well, what a cozy picture you three make. I can see I'm about as necessary in here as lips on a chicken," Shorty grumbled miserably. He maintained a hangdog expression on his weathered face for several long seconds before the smallest signs of a wily grin began to form.

Abby didn't know which was worse—having her father upset by the scene before him or having him pleased by it. Either way it was a no-win situation for everybody. She tapped Guy lightly on the back and, thankfully, he took the hint. His arm dropped from around her and he casually used the free hand to goose Dillon in the ribs. The baby arched his back and giggled at the game he and Guy played, taking turns tickling and laughing. It was no wonder her son had become so attached to the first man who'd been able to get on a toddler's level, roll on the floor and give piggyback rides.

"Hey, Daddy," she said, grazing over the tender moment.

"Good evening, sir. I just dropped by to see if you needed anything and we were all saying hello."

He bent to extend his hand. The two men gripped firmly, the light of friendship beginning to glow in their eyes. She was reminded of the first day Guy had come to their home. The scene outside the laundry room where the bonding had begun, despite her father's reluctance. She tried to recall the envy she'd felt but could only conjure up a warm feeling of appreciation for the companionship Guy had freely offered her father when he'd needed it most. But was Guy's mission to help heal all their hearts from former grief and then leave them with new heartache?

"You're always welcome here, son. Sorry if I've seemed a tad grouchy."

"A tad?" Guy quirked his eyebrows upward at the understatement.

Shorty snorted, the only agreement he was normally willing to give.

"Some days are just harder than others," he admitted. "This business with Sarah being gone is almost over and then we can get back to normal."

Guy wondered what *normal* meant in this home. In his adult years he'd come to understand that the Hardy family was unique in this day of high divorce rates and single-parent homes. A big family, secure in ways that mattered most was definitely becoming an anomaly.

So maybe Shorty was right and *normal* was a family with problems, illness, financial worries and loss. Guy's gut churned from the revelation. How had he failed to understand that before now? How many times had he set away or, worse, driven away a woman who'd come to care for him after he'd helped her out of a tight spot, then dated her for a short while? It wasn't that he didn't respect her feelings, it was just that his mattered more.

Ugh. What a creep.

"Don't mention it, sir." He crossed to the rocker beside the spot where Shorty had positioned his chair. "Do you mind?" He asked Abby's permission to sit with her son. She nodded and he settled carefully, shifted Dillon low so he could cuddle up comfortably and rest against a warm shoulder. The towhead of whisper-fine locks tucked beneath Guy's chin. A perfect fit. Again a burning sensation behind his eyes caught him unaware. He lowered his head, brushed his chin against the blond softness and planted a quiet kiss on Dillon's cheek.

"If you gentlemen will excuse me, I'll put this boy down," Abby offered.

"Oh, please let me hold him a while. I haven't seen my nieces and nephews in months and I could use some Uncle Guy practice." Practice? *Fix* was more like it.

Her brown eyes were puzzled. They held a message he didn't quite understand. She seemed to approve of his closeness with her family, but was he taking it too far? Had he crossed a line? First there was the hug, and then that kiss. *What was he thinking?* And now this need to comfort Dillon. Even Guy had to admit that for a man determined not to have a family of his own, he was sending mixed signals.

Off-limits behavior with a single mom, Casey would say.

He'd clear that up before he left.

"How can I refuse a request like that?" A sad smile curved her pretty lips.

Yep, he had to clear up any seeds of misconception his selfish acts might have planted.

"I'll get back to the practice tests I was sorting over here on the table. Signal when you're ready for me to put him in his crib."

Abby moved to the other side of the room to work in view of where Guy sat rocking Dillon. Her arms and legs were tanned from afternoons of gardening at the playground and helping out in the backyard. She folded one bare foot beneath her bottom and perched on the edge of an oak dining-room chair, colorful stacks scattered across its surface. She punched a button on her portable CD player and an unfamiliar tune punctuated with street lyrics poured from the small speakers.

"Baby girl, how about turning down that racket?"

"It's called hip-hop, Daddy." She rolled her eyes at Guy and lowered the volume but continued to bob her head to the beat.

"What passes for music these days is beyond all adult comprehension," Shorty muttered. "I don't know how the youngsters stand it, do you?"

Ouch! A reminder of the significant age difference between himself and Abby. If Shorty was intentionally going for that point, he'd hit right on the mark.

Guy tried to focus on their conversation as the older man launched into the discussion he'd flatly refused to have only the day before. The details of the home reconstruction were important. The work needed to begin right away if they hoped to have it finished within two weeks. But with the scent of baby powder tickling his nose, the sound of Dillon's soft snoring endearing to Guy's ears and the pleasing sight of Abby engrossed in her work only a few yards away, concentration eluded him.

"So I was thinking I might buy a new Ford and join the NASCAR circuit."

"Good idea," Guy agreed.

"Or maybe pick up a dozen huskies and train for the Iditarod."

"Iditarod?" The old man had finally snapped. He was talking crazy. Guy turned his attention to Shorty and was greeted by dark eyes sparkling beneath bushy gray brows. His thin arms were folded across his chest, his jaw set in that stubborn line that was clearly the family trademark.

"Busted, punk, as the reality TV cops say right before the takedown." He winked, leaned forward and lowered his voice so his words would be masked by the music. "You're still in denial, I see. You cover your feelings for my girl about as well as your hair covers the crown of your head."

He cackled at the insult and patted Guy's arm with a bony hand to indicate no harm was meant. "You better wake up and smell the bacon before it's too late. You'll be gone for good in a few weeks and a girl as special as mine may never cross your path again." He nodded toward the sleeping boy. "Same goes for my precious grandson. I never told this to anybody, but before Phillip deployed I promised him his child would always be in good hands. I'd say that's where he is right now, wouldn't you?"

Guy nodded, lost for words at what was sounding for all the world like Shorty's blessing. He rested his cheek against Dillon's warm head.

Dillon's snores grew louder. "Looks like this little fella is down for the count." Guy chuckled at the baby bear rumbling.

Abby's head popped up, but before she could make a move, Guy stood.

"Keep your seat. I know the way." He cradled the boy close, stepped around Shorty's wheelchair and made his way down the corridor that had become so familiar he could navigate it in the darkness. He settled his precious cargo into the crib, keeping the warmth of a protective hand on Dillon's back until the steady snores resumed.

"You've got quite a fan there, you know." Abby's whisper came from the doorway. He didn't take his eyes off the boy.

"The feeling is mutual. He's adorable, Abby." Just like his mama.

The boards creaked beneath her feet as she stepped closer and stopped beside him. He glanced to his right, looked down into brown eyes that sparkled in the glow of the small night-light he'd fashioned to look like Big Bird.

"Can we talk outside?" she asked softly.

"Sure, I need to get out of your hair so why don't you walk me out to the truck?"

Back in the front room, the two men arranged a drop-off time the next day for building supplies while Abby slid her bare feet into rubber thongs.

She followed him out to the darkened front porch and pulled the door closed behind them.

Before he could take the three concrete steps down to the sidewalk, he felt her hand on his forearm, preventing his progress. This would be the time to set things straight. To apologize for the impetuous kiss and assure her it wouldn't happen again.

"I need to ask a big favor." Her voice was soft. She buffed palms against crossed arms as if fighting off a chill.

"Anything."

Her hands fell limp at her sides. In the dark it was hard to see her face, to read the expression in her sable eyes. Why was she reluctant to speak up, to verbalize this "big favor" she had to ask?

Then it hit him. Money. She was going to ask for money. What else could possibly make her this uncomfortable?

"Abby, what do you need?"

She spoke so softly he couldn't hear.

"I'm sorry, hon, say that again."

She sucked her lungs full of air and let out a tired sigh that made him want to wrap her in his arms till some of his strength passed into her lovely body.

"Would you hug me again?" She didn't

reach out to him. Didn't wiggle an inch. In fact, he was almost positive she expected rejection.

His spirit ached at the idea that she thought he might actually refuse her, that she assumed he'd only do it as a favor. As much as women thrive on reassuring words, seeing was what really enabled believing. His answer came easily. He closed the short space between them, opened his arms. She hesitated. Shy now that she had to make a move of her own.

A LONG MOMENT PASSED. Abby bit the inside of her lip, considered backing out, thankful that the overhead light was out and Guy couldn't see the tears threatening. Being needy was bad enough. Being chicken on top of it was too much for her pride.

Just as her son had done an hour earlier, she shamelessly threw herself against Guy, wound her arms around his waist, pressed her palms flat against his back and pulled herself to him tightly. He folded around her, tucked her beneath his chin and stroked her tired shoulders with sure, firm hands.

"What's all this about?" he murmured into her hair.

She couldn't speak. Between the need lumped up in her throat and the wild pounding of her heart, no breath could whistle through her vocal cords to produce sound.

She'd just have to show him.

CHAPTER THIRTEEN

ABBY SKIMMED HER PALMS across Guy's physique as she slid them away from his back and up the front of his chest. She stood on tiptoe, locked her hands behind his neck and pulled his face within a couple inches of hers.

"I have a revelation for you." She was bold.

"Is that right?"

"Yes, sir." She nodded, drawing out the moment, enjoying the closeness of a man more than she ever thought possible.

"Well…" He leaned in to her. "How about sharing it?" The words were a husky whisper.

"If that kiss had lasted a moment longer, I'd have returned it." She recognized the same quality in her own voice. The feelings were painfully evident, at least to her ears.

He turned his face from side to side, searching the dark confines of the small porch. "I don't see anybody or anything stopping you from doing that now." He stilled, gave her control of the decision.

Her blood raced, pulse resounded in her ears. If she waited another second her knees were going to buckle and he'd have to catch her, or worse help her up off the concrete floor.

She risked the smallest beginning, let her lips softly touch his. He sighed and took the control back as his mouth covered hers, searching her very soul with his kiss. They clung together for long minutes, exchanging tender touches and murmured words.

He pulled away, took a step back and stuffed his hands in his pockets. "Abby, I'm so tempted to do that again. Please go inside before I forget all the reasons why this is a bad idea."

Bad idea?

The sweetest kiss she'd ever experienced was just condensed into two words.

Bad idea!

"You're right, of course." She ducked her head and passed the back of her hand across her lips, still trembling from his touch.

A bolt of lightning split the sky above their

heads. A clap of thunder resounded close enough to set off the alarm in the H&H truck. Guy pulled the keys from his pocket just as the heavens opened and released enough rain to turn the narrow driveway into a new tributary of the Colorado.

"I'll call you," he yelled over the torrential pounding on the roof, and made a run for it.

Abby's sinking spirits lifted at the sight of Guy's drenched body struggling with the door that wouldn't open until the alarm was disengaged, something that seemed to take several tries before he was successful. By the time he scrambled into the truck, he was soaked to the skin.

She opened the screen door, stepped inside the quiet house and watched as the man who'd just called their kiss a bad idea disappeared into the downpour.

IF, AS TEXANS CLAIMED, the Lone Star State was God's country, then Austin had turned into His swimmin' hole! The rest of the week it rained nonstop. The thoroughfares flooded; the mayor asked all but emergency vehicles to stay off the streets and naturally, school was canceled. Critical days of test preparation were lost and would have to be recovered somehow. It was makeup work that weighed heavily on Abby's mind since her kids' placement in the year-end skills tests was a direct reflection on her teaching ability.

Then there was the misery of being confined to the stuffy house when they'd all rather be outside, Dillon digging in his sandbox, Daddy making his daily commute to visit Mama and Abby doing the hundred things that needed to be accomplished that week. The weather would set her back much more than the couple of days it lasted because it would be many more before the earth dried out enough to continue the playground project.

Mother's Day was closing in. Instead of being the happy celebration it had been in the past, it was looming on the calendar, a deadline with so much riding on it.

Friday morning the phone jangled at 6:00 a.m.

"Who is making calls at this hour?"

"I've got it, Daddy," Abby called toward her parents' bedroom as she cinched the belt of her cotton robe and reached for the portable phone mounted just inside the kitchen door.

Who indeed? Only the rehab center would be calling so early, though she wasn't about to say so. She planted her feet, grabbed the handset and prepared for the worst.

"Hello?"

"Good morning, sunshine!"

"Guy?" Her voice rose.

"Why do you sound so surprised?"

She glanced at the kitchen clock for confirmation.

"Well, it's barely six and I was afraid it might be the hospital calling."

"Oh, I'm so sorry, hon. I wouldn't worry you like that even for a moment."

"It's okay. What's up that has you on the phone so early?"

"First, I wanted to apologize for not calling to check on you for a few days. I've been really busy with a Mother's Day deadline of my own, but I wanted to make it a priority to see if you needed anything this morning."

"I need the sun to come out today and dry up all this water so I can get something done this weekend. Now we'll never be ready for the dedication." She sounded whiny. Well, shoot, she had a right to be disappointed. The results of her hard work were probably being washed away as they spoke.

Guy chuckled on his end of the phone.

"Please tell me what you find amusing about that."

"Get your jeans on and I'll be there in fifteen minutes. The water has subsided on the major roads so we can go for a ride and I'll show you."

"I can't go off and leave Dillon alone with Dad, and I have to be at school by noon." The rain had let up overnight and teachers had been asked to report to work by midday.

"We'll take Dillon with us and I'll have you back home by nine. I'll treat us all to a hearty breakfast at Flapjack Heaven. Those genius Carlton brothers just opened up their hundredth location not too far from the new playground and they're giving away all kinds crazy of prizes to celebrate. I thought I might get some ideas for the picnic this weekend."

Abby dragged a hand through her tangled mess of curls. She knew she should decline, but the fluttering against her ribs at the thought of how Dillon would enjoy an outing with Guy, especially after a couple of days of being shut in the house, was too much to resist.

Her inner voice called her bluff. *Who are you fooling, kiddo? Don't blame the desire to be with a man who recently called your kiss a "bad idea" on your innocent son. Guy works on a Mother's Day project and you melt. He offers you a ride to breakfast and you start fluffing your hair. Get a grip. The man is a rescuer and a do-gooder. Let him exercise his savior complex and then get back to the business of taking care of your family.*

"Okay." She stood and set her coffee cup in the sink. "You talked me into it. Give me time to get Dillon dressed and twist my hair into a knot and we'll be ready to go.

"Perfect. And Abby?"

"Yes?"

"Leave your hair down."

BREAKFAST WAS A JOY. Abby couldn't remember when she'd had so much fun watching her son mutilate a meal. His stubby fingers were gummy with butter, syrup and pancake. His face was equally gooey but he'd managed to put away a plateful of silver-dollar flapjacks in record time.

Dillon played with the remnants of his breakfast, swirled his fingers on his sticky plate then held an offering aloft. Abby watched from across the table, astonished each time Guy accepted a bite, smacked his lips with a loud "Yum, yum, yum!" making Dillon squeal with delight.

"What?" Guy asked her when she smiled at him.

"You're incredible with my son. I have to confess I'm a bit reluctant to accept most of his mealtime offerings."

"You washed his hands before we were seated, and he basically had the same thing on his plate that I had on mine." Guy defended Dillon. "He's learning to share, to be generous. I wouldn't dream of discouraging him."

"You're a big-hearted person."

"I had great role models."

"Your sisters again, I suppose?"

"Oh, no!" He smiled and rolled his eyes. "The gaggle taught me lots of things, that's for sure. But I learned generosity from the men in our family. My dad and my eleven uncles all have hearts for giving. When Dad was raising the seed money for Hearth and Home it was our family who stepped up first. They believed in my dad and wouldn't let him fail. I credit my parents' siblings for the success we have today." He took a sip of hot coffee and seemed to consider what he said next. His gaze locked on hers. "Abby, family is the most important thing in life to me. There's *nothing* I wouldn't do to protect the ones I love."

She returned his stare. In the bottom of her stomach, her breakfast turned to stone as she interpreted the message he'd just delivered. He would line up against anybody who tried to come between him and family. And that included her. How many times and how many ways did he have to tell her he had all the family he needed?

Dillon cocked his arm back and flung the last bite of mushed-up pancake. It sailed several feet, frapped against the wall beside them and skipped a sticky trail downward till it came to rest on the tile floor.

"Wow, with that arm our boy could be a closer for the Astros," Guy joked, then took his napkin and scooped up the mess. "Think we should give him a hunk of biscuit to see if he can do that again?"

But Abby was already focused on cleaning Dillon's squirming fingers with a wet nap. Anything to keep from thinking about Guy's warning. And wasn't that exactly what it had been? A warning that his family was precious to him and he'd protect them at all costs. That was an admirable quality in a man. She should be impressed. Instead she felt threatened, alone, on the outside looking in.

He stood. "Here, let me help." He slipped strong hands against Dillon's sides, scooped him out of the high chair and held him dangling at arm's length so she could wipe him down. The room filled with the sound of her son's bubbly laughter as he kicked thick-soled sneakers and enjoyed the game.

"Guy! Wheet, wheet!"

"Little buddy, as flattering as it is to me and the blue jays, we need to teach you some more words. I'm gonna bring some treats tomorrow so you can feed the animals and learn their names."

"Animals?" Abby looked up from her effort to remove maple syrup from Dillon's chubby legs.

"Sure. The petting zoo is always a favorite."

"You mean you haven't canceled the picnic?"

"You don't think we cancel H&H events just because of a little rain, do you?"

"A *little* rain? Even by Texas standards this week's rainfall has been a gully washer."

"And that's why we always have a backup plan for our employee events. We go all out to show them our appreciation. It's part of what makes our work atmosphere so special." He cuddled Dillon in the crook of a strong arm and tossed several bills on the table.

"Backup plan, huh?" She slung the ever-present diaper bag over her shoulder.

"The Hardy family is famous for our backup plans. We don't like to let anything come between us and a deadline. Tomorrow you'll witness it on a corporate scale, but right now you're about to see what the Warden is capable of on her own."

Abby took a step away from Guy and drew her chin to her chest, scared turtle style.

"Oh, my. What could Casey possibly be up to in this weather?"

What indeed!

Ten minutes later Abby got her first exposure to the work of Casey Hardy when she was racing ahead of a deadline. The half acre of land for the playground looked as if it were being treated as a hazardous-substance spill site!

"What in the…" Abby was literally lost for words. The last of the drizzle had stopped during their breakfast. Morning sun angled through the clouds and glinted off the slick parking lot. She climbed from the truck and stood transfixed, staring at the sight while Guy helped Dillon from his car seat.

An enormous navy-blue tent any traveling circus would be proud to own had been erected. Industrial-size generators powered pumps that blew air into the top of the protective covering, then sucked streams of water around and past the booms strung end to end to prevent leakage beneath the tent. The thing moved with a breathing motion like those big blow-up moon walks kids loved at the school carnivals.

"This is why I laughed when you said you wouldn't be ready for the dedication on Mother's Day. Casey never leaves anything to chance. You put her second in command and, by golly, she's not going to fall short of the goal."

"How…? What…?" Abby was dazed, downright amazed by the sight before her. And even more so considering *nobody* had phoned to tell her this was going on.

"Come on." He touched her arm, gently urged her toward the flap of canvas folded back to mark the entrance. "All the answers are waiting inside, so go see for yourself."

Lively music poured from the opening as they approached. A female sang along, the effort heartfelt and robust even if off-key. Abby quirked an eyebrow at Guy, unable to hold back a smile.

"Yep, it's a family curse," he said, reading her mind. "None of us can carry a tune in a bucket except for our mom. She has an angel's voice and the rest of us croak like bullfrogs."

Abby ducked her head, stepped through the opening and stood as if hypnotized, wide eyed, stunned. Floodlights suspended upon tall poles filled the area with artificial daylight. The whirling blades of several huge cage fans blew a mechanical breeze that stirred the grass and the flowering plants, heavy with blooms sure to burst with a cornucopia of color just in time for Mother's Day.

She risked a step forward, expecting to sink into soggy soil. But the ground beneath her feet held firm, completely dry, as if the soaking rains had never touched this quarter acre of Texas. In the center of the playground Casey worked atop a tall ladder, her back to the new arrivals, unaware of their presence. She sang with gusto, unconscious or unconcerned for the screeching quality of her voice. She fished a tool from the leather belt fastened low around her hips and tightened the chain for the swing dangling before her.

Abby moved closer, noted the gleaming paint on each refurbished piece of equipment, the benches restored with new planks rubbed to a smooth finish, the colorful walk-way laid of mix-and-match tiles that led to an arbor-covered sandbox complete with an artist's backdrop of blue skies, fluffy white clouds and a floating castle.

A lot of effort had been expended in the past couple of days. A lot of effort. Almost everything she'd intended to do had been completed. There was hardly anything left for her to work on.

As with the day Guy had materialized at her home and taken over the things she and her dad had planned to accomplish together, she felt loss well up and sting her eyes. She was unnecessary. Redundant. Replaced. How could she ever claim this small plot of land as a tribute to her husband? Her plan had been followed to the T but her fingerprints were absent from the finished product.

"Rebecca Thelma Casey," Guy called above the fans and his baby sister's singing. "You never cease to amaze me, girl."

She turned a wide smile on her brother, dropped without fear off the tall stepladder and strode their way, her arms outstretched to fold Abby into a hug.

"It's about time you got here," she teased. "I'm badly in need of your expert guidance. I managed to keep the place from floating away, and I got all the little things done, but now it's time to talk about the sculpture garden and how you want the area around the pecan tree to shape up.

"Well?" She kept one arm snug around Abby's shoulders as they turned a slow circle together, surveying the results of her hard work. Then she wisely left Abby to consider a response, snatching up Dillon and playfully jiggling him into a fit of happy shrieks.

Guy moved close, put a warm hand on the small of Abby's back. "So, what do you think?"

She lowered her voice and turned away from Casey's hearing. "At the risk of sounding ungrateful, I think your extremely efficient little sister has just managed me out of my own project."

"Ahhhhh." He nodded, understanding. "That's another family curse. We don't just help out. We take over. Casey's still gotta learn how to temper that tendency but thankfully I've mastered it."

Abby spewed laughter, loud, unexpected and uncontrolled. She leaned forward from the waist, rested her hands on her knees and gave in to the irony of his ridiculous claim. Casey had called it on the nose when she'd said her brother had a savior complex. Yeah, that was it, aptly put for sure!

"Oh, that's the best laugh I've had in weeks."

He pushed his lips into an exaggerated pout. "I beg your pardon. Is that your way of saying you disagree?"

"That's my way of saying you're sadly mistaken if you believe for one minute that you've mastered your need to do extreme favors that rescue damsels in distress."

His mouth pressed into a flat line. "Hmmmm, I guess you could have something there. But I'm not as bad as I used to be. I have made progress, I know I have."

"You mean the way you've helped out with our house and practically become a member of my family is pulling back on the stick for you?"

"Okay, okay, you've made your point." He held his palms up, warding off any further dispute.

"What are you two muttering about over here?" Casey had joined them with Dillon settled on her slender hip. He was more than happy to be in the arms of the woman who showered his blond head with soft kisses and goosed him in the back producing involuntary giggles.

"Your brother was giving me the family history on getting carried away with good deeds to the point of taking over. He seems to think he has that trait under control."

Oddly, Casey didn't crack up at the notion as Abby had. Instead she looked hard at Guy and nodded. "I think he has, actually. Compared to circumstances in the past where he ingratiated himself so quickly and thoroughly that ladies tried to drag him to the altar, I'd say he's come a long way." She looped her free arm through Guy's, pulled him close and their stunning blue eyes locked. "He's much better about stating his intentions up front and sticking with them for the sake of the family. Aren't you, bro?"

"I have a way to go, that's for sure, but I try not to focus so hard on the goal that I lose perspective on how I get there."

"Well said." Casey nodded her head then turned to Abby. "And while we're on this subject, I hope you aren't offended that I took so much liberty here. But I knew your time was running out and this weather would probably stop you in your tracks. We've had a similar situation during minor construction in the past and I knew this would work. So, I called in the cavalry before the weather set in, put up the tent and went to work."

"You could have called me, too. I've been shut in the house for the past couple of days when I could have been helping."

"Yeah, and instead of looking rested and beautiful, which really annoys me by the way," Casey complimented Abby with a wink, "and being caught up with those stacks of school papers Guy says you always have, you'd be worn to a frazzle and wouldn't have enough stamina left to get through the rest of this deal."

"She makes a good point," Guy agreed with Casey.

"As usual," she added, complimenting herself.

Guy stepped away from his sister, took

Abby by the elbow and guided her to the small pecan tree surrounded by a low white fence.

"Now, as she said, Casey's left a number of important decisions and details for you alone. So why don't you tell us what you had in mind for right here."

Abby stared at the sapling. Tried to conjure up Phillip's picture in her mind's eye. Nothing. Nothing would come. How could she have been his constant companion and not be able to envision him standing before her now? She looked at Dillon. At this age there were no signs of Phillip in their son's features.

She squeezed her eyes tight, dropped her chin to her chest and tried to recall the most simple of Kodak moments in their lives; the senior prom, their wedding day, the first time she saw him in uniform. She could see the backdrops, the colors of their clothes and her own happy face. But Phillip's was a blur.

The tears flowed, seeped through her lashes and trickled down her face. A slow dribble became a rush of emotion. She struggled to hold back the sobs but the force of the release shook her body. A strong arm settled gently around her shoulders, turned her slowly, pressed her to a solid chest. In the comfort of Guy's embrace she crumbled, but he held her secure, pressed her to him for warmth, for strength.

He let her cry.

GUY PULLED ABBY TIGHT against him, listened to her heart breaking and felt his crumble right along with it.

Even in death he's still her husband. She adores him with all her might. How much more obvious can it be that there's no more room for love in her life. No room in her heart for me.

CHAPTER FOURTEEN

POSSIBLY FOR THE FIRST TIME in his thirty-eight years, Guy didn't have a single clue as to how to handle a situation involving a female. But then the woman in his arms was someone he'd never expected to find. Hadn't even *wanted* to find. And now, in perfect and ironic timing, here she was. Pressed close in her grief, oblivious to the wild drumming in Guy's chest, so great was the emptiness, the loss she still mourned.

Abby Cramer was faithful. She was loyal. She was true. She was a woman he knew he could love.

Could love? Correction. Loved.

Loved with his mind, body and soul.

He'd spent his entire life dating women easy to get over. He didn't want to get over Abby.

I've found the one my heart loves. The realization should have stunned him. It was so far off the mark that it should have left him breathless with anxiety. It was such a departure from his life plan that he should have collapsed inward upon himself, no stronger than the sweet girl he cradled against his chest.

Instead there was an intense joy he'd never expected to know mingled with an unbelievable pain he'd intentionally avoided. The discord of feelings surged through his veins, pounded with his pulse. He bent low, folded Abby closer, pressed his face to her hair and murmured soothing words.

She lifted her head, tilted it back, allowing him to see the unbelievable depth of the sorrow in her eyes. He wanted to kiss away the sadness, tell her he'd chase away the tears as far as the east is from the west. Make her smile again one day if she'd only have him.

"I'm sorry," she choked on the whispered words. "Before Phillip died, I had no inkling loss could hurt physically, be so brutal. This is like a terminal disease with no hope of relief. I couldn't bear to go through this again. Ever."

Guy had some small measure of understanding. The woman he'd only just discovered he loved was telling him her heartbreak was permanent. She would never risk loving again.

Did he merely accept what she believed couldn't be changed, or did he gamble everything to prove her wrong?

"I hate to disturb you two because I can see something private is going on over there, but it feels like Mansfield Dam just broke in this kid's shorts." Casey spoke from a respectful distance, both humor and concern laced her voice. "If we don't get him changed soon, all the effort I made the last three days to keep the flooding off this plot of land is all for naught."

Abby passed her palms over her face, swiping away the telltale trails of the emotional encounter, and stepped around Guy to reach for her son.

"Here, give him to me."

"I'll get his bag from the truck," Guy offered.

Casey handed Dillon over carefully so as not to disturb his diaper. Abby slung him over her hip without concern and headed toward the far side of the tent.

"I'll over to the community center. There's a ladies' room in the lobby with a changing table just inside the door."

"Sure thing. I'll knock and hand the bag through to you." He watched the mother and child that he wanted to claim for his own disappear from his sight, then turned to his errand.

"Man, you are tore up from the floor up, bro."

He didn't have to look at her face to know Casey wore a big smile. Neither did he need to ask what she meant.

Simply put, he was in a world of trouble.

SATURDAY MORNING dawned as different from the rest of the week as Texas is from the polar ice cap. The springtime sun shot into the crystal-blue skies over Austin, pulling steamy rays of heat from the pavement, mirages shimmering through wavy lines.

Abby had accepted weeks ago that Guy was a man who wouldn't take no for an answer. It wasn't that he was pushy or controlling, just determined when it came to doing something he knew would make life easier for another person. So when he'd insisted on accompanying the family to the rehab center to start the day's outing, Abby had agreed without argument. She'd struggled with the logistics of how she'd manage her son and both parents at the same time. Having them together under their own roof after her mom was released was going to be difficult enough. Taking them all on a picnic outing for the first time was probably more than she could handle by herself without some practice.

Her folks would be mortified at her true feelings but the childhood home where she'd once been nurtured and comforted had become a place filled with anxiety and unexpected stressors. She was on her own, the caregiver for a demanding three where she'd once been the mother to a precious one. She'd heard about the sandwich generation, but weren't they supposed to be the fifty-something baby boomers? Those decades-older people who found themselves taking care of aging parents as they prepared for retirement. At this rate she'd never make it that far; she'd collapse under the weight of responsibility before she ever made it to thirty, much less her golden years.

"Guy's here!" her dad shouted from the sentry position he'd taken by the front window. "Let's go!"

He'd been giddy as a groom since Guy had hatched his plan. The idea of breaking their patient out of the center for the day had her dad more revved up than a Formula One pace car.

"Are you sure we're not putting your mother's final release from rehab at risk?"

Abby opened the front door and waited for Guy, her belly swarming with nervous jitters at his approach.

"Dad, if there was any chance of that, we wouldn't be doing this. Dr. Cabot assured me this would be a well-deserved reward for Mom after all her physical therapy as well as good training for us on how we'll need to help her when she comes home."

"Everybody ready?" The man who'd unknowingly won her heart took the front steps in one leap and reached for the screen-door handle.

"Been ready since first light. What took you so long, Roy Rogers?" Shorty groused.

But her dad's voice was charged with a new energy. She half expected him to get up out of his chair and make the trip out to the van under his own steam. The excitement over an entire day with the woman he treasured above all else was an aura surrounding him, a glow that pulsed with the very beat of his heart.

Will there ever again be a man in my life who feels that way about me?

"Good morning to you, too, Shorty," Guy laughed, picking up on the fact that the still-grouchy tone was for show only. "Let's get everybody loaded up and then I thought we'd take the scenic route, maybe drive around the campus a few times and see if we can't find a traffic jam or some roadwork."

Her dad made a fist, squinted and tried his best to look menacing. "You delay picking up my Sarah by as much as five minutes and I'll put a knot in the middle of that bald spot on your noggin."

Guy's eyes grew round with exaggerated fear. "Abby, I sure hope you and Dillon are ready. I'm prepared for any eventuality with the Admiral and the Warden being in the same place at the same time but I hadn't factored Evander Holyfield into the mix. Let's not risk it, okay?"

The quick wink and his confident smile telegraphed so much: conspiracy, fun, understanding and something else she was almost afraid to name. It was as if he'd asked to carry the heavy load today, to take on some of her responsibility.

To be trusted with her precious burdens.

She loved Guy Hardy. And in the wink of that charming blue eye, she made a decision. The man could never return her feelings, didn't want to. But just for today she would pretend, if only for a short while, that he was the rock she'd never known, might never have.

"HOW ON EARTH did you manage to pull this off?"

Abby strolled the covered section of the Expo Center grounds with Guy and hundreds of others as they meandered through acres of games, crafts and activities designed to offer a challenging distraction at every age and ability level. Dillon had been eager to go to Casey when she'd met them at the handicapped parking area and immediately insisted on seeing to Sarah and Shorty's barbecue lunch.

"I won't discount the fact that having money to invest in the community buys a lot of cooperation from local officials who struggle with dwindling budgets and legal handcuffs." He reluctantly admitted this, the furrows between his brows further telegraphing what must have been a significant figure to produce the results his employees were enjoying. "But we've been working on this event since our initial groundbreaking."

"This has been in the works all those months?" Abby sipped refreshing pink lemonade and marveled at the wisdom of Hearth and Home for including employee recognition in their long-range planning.

"Sure. We won't turn a shovel of dirt in Galveston for three more months but I've already got Casey looking into sites for our first appreciation event."

Guy's mention of Galveston turned the sweet drink as bitter as bile in her mouth.

Once again the rush of reality swept her thinking, making it nearly impossible to imagine for even a day that anything lasting could happen between them. The man who was the rock of her daydream would soon shift and disappear, no different than sand beneath the constant tide.

She had to think of something else or risk pouting like a preteen the rest of the day. With Guy close behind, she left the stream of foot traffic in search of some quiet. At the periphery of the fairgrounds they stopped at a private spot and leaned comfortably against a whitewashed corral-style fence.

"You said Casey is doing that event planning. I thought you coordinated everything until the store was ready to turn over to her?"

"That's always been true in the past, but my little sister has too much time on her hands right now so I'm loading her up with some agreement negotiations and construction licenses. That's a little outside of her area of responsibility but the girl's never known a boundary in her life. Challenging her to stretch a bit is like asking Lance Armstrong if he minds cycling an extra mile."

"Is everybody in your family as competitive as you two?" She was glad for the shift in conversation, needed time to push past the thought of Guy's imminent departure from Austin.

From her life.

Guy paused for a moment, then answered.

"All the girls are extremely goal-oriented but that's part of our family culture. Casey is another matter altogether." He smiled at the understatement. "She came out of the gate looking for a challenge. Since the day she won her first spelling bee she has refused to let the eight-year difference between us be an excuse not to best me. When I got my MBA she was still in high school, but she was already warning me she'd go me one better so Dad would know there was nothing magical about being a man that uniquely qualified me to step into the CEO role. She got her master black belt in Six Sigma while she was still in college, believing that would be her springboard into an executive position."

"And was she right?"

"Of course! Now she's got some wild ideas about revolutionizing our corporate security system. Why else do you think she keeps sneaking into our new stores trying to trip me up? It drives me nuts!"

"Even so, it's obvious how much you love your sister."

"Oh, it goes beyond family ties. I think I respect her as much as I love her."

"I guess Casey's brand of steamroller drive and talent are what you find most attractive in a woman, right?"

He took the sweating cup of melting ice cubes from her hand and balanced it atop a fence post. Then he reached for her hand, turned her to face him and leaned down so she would hear his quiet voice over the noise level of the open-sided tents in the distance.

"There was a time when that might have been an accurate statement. But as I get older, I've gained the wisdom to look past outward signs, outward efforts and instead see the good deep inside people. That's why the geodes mean so much to me. They are a tangible symbol of the buried treasure in each of us. They remind me that I'm lucky to be a help to others."

"And 'others' just happens to be women more often than not?"

"Ouch!" He clutched his chest, pulled an imaginary dagger from his heart. "I see Casey's been talking while she works."

"Oh, as if Daddy hasn't given you color commentary on every major event in my life."

Guy chuckled. "I admit I've probably heard more about your school years that I have a right to know. But Shorty is so proud of you, he can't help bragging a little."

"If I didn't know better I'd think my dad and your sister have conspired against us. They both seem to be working overtime, turning up the heat with stories designed to make each of us hightail it the other way."

GUY WATCHED with fascination, mesmerized as Abby shoved curls back from her forehead and swiped either cheek where rosy, warm skin was responding to the sultry day. She puffed breath upward, reached behind her head, twisted her hair into a knot and held it off her neck.

"Speaking of heat…" He dipped his hand into the cup of melting ice, withdrew a chilly chunk and held it up between thumb and forefinger. "I have just the thing to cool you off." He knew his grin gave away his intentions.

Her gaze flicked left to right, presumably for an avenue of escape. "Thank you, but that won't be necessary." She held her palms out.

"Oh, but I think it will be," he threatened, inching closer.

"You wouldn't dare." She sounded tough, but took a step away just in case, not so sure he wouldn't follow through.

He lowered his voice, growled from his throat.

"Don't tempt me, pretty lady. Back home I'm known as the Snowman for good reason. No sister ever escaped a winter assault or a summer meltdown!"

She crept backward, a glint of playful trepidation in her brown eyes. "Don't do it, Guy Hardy," she warned.

He matched her motions, easing forward as she eased back. He fixed her with a beguiling smile. "We can do this the hard way and make a lot of fuss that the people way over there will notice, or you can stand still and take it like the cowgirl you claim to be."

She stood her ground, didn't move. Her eyes narrowed. The muscles in her jaw flexed with determination and Sarah Reagan's daughter stood before him as stubborn as a borrowed mule. At that moment it was not difficult to envision Abby as a champion barrel racer.

Ahhhh, he was seeing a new dimension. He'd never issued a challenge to her before, assuming that was not her style. Why, she'd even baited him moments earlier with her question about Casey's steamrolling. Seemed Abby had the force of some heavy equipment in her makeup after all.

"Tell you what." He decided to test her a bit. "You let me see just how tough you are and you can call payback anytime it suits you."

She threaded both hands through her blond hair, pressed it high atop her head, exposing the fair skin of her neck. "Bring it on, Alexander Theodore Guy," she whispered, then closed her eyes and angled her head in coy submission.

The offering of her lovely throat stirred his senses, shook his resolve not to initiate another kiss. Maybe he could risk a small one on that neck so artfully etched with character and strength.

"Well, what are you waiting for?" she interrupted his thought. The question and the mirth in her voice were meant to tease, to find out if he'd started something he had no intention of finishing.

This time he was the one glancing around to ensure the moment was a private one. With nobody in sight, he stepped close, reached out with the melting chunk of ice, held it several inches above the skin where he was so tempted to press his lips and let cold droplets fall.

She shivered at the contact, tensed and then relaxed. Gooseflesh prickled on either side of her spine as the moisture drizzled downward to disappear beneath the collar of her pale blue oxford-cloth cotton shirt.

He closed his fingers around the ice, the warmth of his hand turning the drips to a steady trickle.

"Mmmmmmm, that's actually very nice," Abby admitted. She pressed her shoulders back, permitting entry of the rivulet that traced her spine, a darkening streak of dampness.

"That's not supposed to be your response."

"I know. Not what you expected, huh?"

"Not even close," he admitted. "Where are the screams, the struggles, the threats of payback?"

"You're about eight years too late for that. The stables where I worked in high school were pretty spartan. In the summer a cup of ice was the only way to cool off unless you wanted to take a dip in the horse trough." She raised her head, light flashing in her cocoa-brown eyes. "Sorry to disappoint you on the screams and struggles, but I'll definitely take you up on the payback when you least expect it."

"Then I might as well get my money's worth." He dropped the chunk of ice down the neck of her shirt, pressed his hand over the lump it made where it settled at the waistband of her jeans and ground the chill into the small of her back.

He was rewarded with a whoop of laughter and an effort to squirm away. He caught her around the middle, wrapped her tight and pulled her against him.

"Oh no you don't," he laughed, enjoying the horseplay.

At the precise moment he'd intended to release her so she could fish the ice cube from beneath her shirt, Abby tipped her head back. She looked up into his face, then closed her eyes as if giving him control. Giving him permission.

He stared down. As motionless and dense as the fence post they'd been leaning against. Without a thought for propriety or permission, he dipped his face and covered her sweet mouth with his.

CHAPTER FIFTEEN

WITH HER EYES tightly closed to ease the wild reality that was Guy's kiss, Abby's mind was a whirlwind of senses. The prickle of a half day's whiskers where his mouth met hers, the uncontrollable thumping of hearts pressed close, the small sighs they exchanged.

And the physical sensations were accompanied by a blur of questions. *Will Guy see this as another mistake? Am I a fool to care for a man who has no intention of returning my love?* And the most important question nagged the loudest. *Why do I get this glimpse of love when it's only going to be taken away again?*

Her confusion deepened along with the kiss. How could there be so much pleasure mingled with fears of hurting? Phillip had already been taken away from her.

Phillip.

She pulled away, stared into unforgettable

azure-blue eyes that held no inkling of remorse, no signs of regret for the kiss.

Guy leaned down, pressed his forehead to hers and uttered a single word. "What?"

There were a thousand possible answers. Which response was she bold enough to give?

"Do you think it's wrong—"

"No," he interrupted, cutting her off with another brief kiss. "This is not wrong, Abby and it's not a mistake. As a matter of fact, it may be the most right thing I've ever done. I've spent the adult years of my life wanting women to move on as soon as they made an effort to sink roots with me. And now I understand how they felt." He gave her lips yet another whisper-soft kiss. "Is that the answer you wanted to hear?"

She couldn't hold back a small smile at the unexpected confession.

"Actually, that wasn't going to be my question at all." She noted the quick intake of his breath as he realized his mistake. Was he sorry he'd tipped his hand?

"But thanks for sharing," she continued. "Actually, I was wondering if it's wrong to care for a man when you promised your heart to another forever."

Guy's forehead still touched hers, but he turned his face slightly, averted his eyes.

They were pressed so closely that she felt the change in Guy right away. It was as if the wind had abandoned his sails. She heard him exhale, felt the warm rush of breath against her cheek.

FOREVER. She'd given her heart away forever.

He was falling deeper and deeper in love with Abby Cramer and it was a foolish waste of time. Why had Fate led him to a love that was unattainable?

"I realize I should be able to give you an older and wiser perspective, Abby." The statement was meant to sound ironic, instead it was just sad to his ears. "The fact is I haven't experienced what you have, so I don't think I'm the one to give you counsel on that particular subject. But after thirty-eight years on this planet what I do know for sure is that loss is part of life and life still manages to go on. Hearts heal, we get blessed with second chances and we sometimes find the next love is sweeter."

Abby straightened, dropped her hands to her sides and took a step back. A step away from his embrace, as if she was finished with the moment. Finished with him.

"That's what Mama and Daddy keep telling me."

"Well, from what I've seen they're pretty smart folks."

"Yeah, and they've had each other for almost fifty years. What do they know about loss?"

He reached for her hand, pulled her close.

"Maybe it's not my place to remind you of this, Abby, but the day we laid the new laundry-room tile, Shorty told me that they lost several babies before they were blessed with you. I'd say they know quite a lot about losing something precious and having the next love be sweeter for the surviving, wouldn't you?"

She ducked her head.

"How shameful that I've never thought of it that way. And how embarrassing."

"I wouldn't call it shameful. You've simply lacked their personal perspective, just like I lack yours. But as long as you learn from it, don't you think you should forgive yourself? I certainly think you should."

As he stroked the pad of his thumb lightly across the back of her soft hand, he couldn't help but wonder if in giving Abby absolution he was really saying it was okay for him to accept the same pardon. His insistence on having relationships his way or no way was certainly much more to be ashamed of than what this kindhearted young woman had done. What an illustration of the difference in their thinking that she felt guilty as soon as she recognized the behavior while he had spent years feeling justified.

Until today.

"You asked me a question. I'd like to answer it if you'll look at me."

She raised her eyes but kept her face downcast.

"No, that's not good enough." He put his index finger beneath her chin, tipped her head back. "Much better. While I still have you all to myself for a few minutes I want to see your beautiful face."

He'd come to know the slight tilt of her

blond head and the squint of her eyes that
said she wasn't sure she deserved a compliment. He would gladly fork over any amount
of money to change that.

"You asked if it's right to care for another
when you've given your heart away."

She nodded.

"Let me answer you this way. Each time
your mother carried a new life I feel certain
she gave her whole heart to that unborn child.
And each time the promise of that life ended
she must have felt some piece of herself die
along with it."

The brown depths glistened.

"Don't you think that's probably true? Even
for somebody as tough as the Admiral?"

Abby smiled and nodded, as he'd hoped
she would.

He squeezed her hand, a reassurance. "But
all that pain hasn't kept her from loving you
desperately, even if she's not the most adept
person at showing it. I've spent hours sitting
with your dad beside Sarah's bed these past
weeks hearing the stories of your life that
Shorty's already shared in great detail."

"Why didn't you stop her?" Abby scrunched her pretty ash-blond brows together in dismay.

"That never even crossed my mind. I just pretended I was hearing every single word for the first time so she'd keep talking, entertaining your father. It was adorable to watch the two of them."

Abby rolled her eyeballs and tried without success to pull her hands free. "Guy, you poor thing. How boring for you to be captive to her lectures." Sympathy was etched in Abby's tone.

He chuckled at her discomfort. "Quite the contrary. I know a little something about the love and pride a mother has for a daughter. Abby, that pride is undeniable in Sarah when she talks about you. Shorty may believe you're his baby girl, but I guarantee the woman who carried you next to her heart for those nine months is the one who knows it for certain."

Abby's mouth popped open and rounded into a kissable pink O that made him want to touch his lips to hers again. But he didn't dare until he'd finished what he'd started.

"I got a bit off track, but my point is this.

It's not only natural, it's part of the healing process to love again. And to want to *kiss* again." He winked to lighten the serious moment. "Even when that first, precious commitment has ended in death."

She was still for so long that Guy feared he might have blown it. Then she reached with her free hand for the cup holding the melting ice. He gave it to her.

"That's kinda what Casey said to me."

"Really. When was that?"

She pressed her lips together but her eyes sparkled with some secret humor. "Oh, in the same conversation when she told me what a notorious ladies' man you are."

It was his turn to be mortified over family musings. "Please, don't keep me in suspense. What wisdom could the Warden possibly have on the subject of recovering from loss?"

"She said my heart was mending and that it might even be time for me to consider dating again."

He'd throttle Casey for sure over that suggestion! Better yet, he'd send the little troublemaker to Galveston on Monday to spend eight hours filing permits at the courthouse.

It was a chore generally delegated to a college intern. But his busybody sister was about to earn some of her obscene salary standing in a long line while she considered her meddling ways.

"Is that a fact?"

"Yes, it is. And here comes possibility right now."

She pointed across the way where colorful rigs destined for the Luedecke Arena were lined up to enter the Expo Center. "That red gooseneck with the Rockin' R emblem is owned by a guy I used to rodeo with, Garrett Ramsey. He's quite the steer-roping champ these days. I've always admired the way that man sits a horse."

Guy noted the approval in her voice, longed to believe she felt something like that about him. He kicked at a dirt clod with a fancy boot that had never seen the inside of a barn, let alone the inside of a stirrup. It had been a long time since he'd felt the need to compete on any level with another man. At least this one was flesh and blood and not a loving memory, so the playing field was level.

Sort of. How did a drugstore cowboy, as

Shorty was so fond of calling him, compete
with the real thing? Especially when Real
Thing was probably a dozen years younger?
Guy rubbed his hand over his head, felt his
thinning crown, knew there had to be another
way to rope that doggy. And hopefully a way
that wouldn't put him in a body cast!

"Do you think you can contain your excitement long enough to join me for a barbecue
sandwich?"

"Sure," she agreed. "Just lead the way."

Intent on having Abby's undivided attention once again, he pulled her along in the
direction of the food tents. A splash of icy
water made contact with the back of his H&H
shirt, seeped through the fabric and plastered
it to his skin. He hunched his shoulders and
sucked in his breath.

"Oh, did I mention I was calling payback?"
Abby asked as laughter erupted from the core
of her body and bubbled up like a natural
spring. Even as gooseflesh prickled everywhere the water clung, Guy had to admit that
the sound of her joy was without doubt one
of the sweetest he'd ever heard.

"How cool is it that all those smokin' hot cowboys showed up today?" Casey balanced Dillon on one hip with her elbow crooked expertly around him. Abby marveled at her son, completely at ease in this place crowded with strangers, having no need at the moment for his mama's comfort. Casey's other arm was raised, her hand shielding her eyes against the midday glare of the sun while she focused on the long stream of pickup trucks and horse trailers winding their way through the entry gate.

"Casey, my dear, you have a couple hundred guests to attend to. Worry about men crazy enough to sit bareback on mean broncs another day."

"Mrs. Reagan, I'd normally defer to an older woman's recommendation especially when she's accustomed to giving orders and having them followed." She winked at Abby's mother. "Not unlike myself." The two were definitely chiseled from the same granite. "But it's not every day that I find myself a stone's throw from a bunch of guys in boots and jeans who want nothing more than eight seconds on a filly whose primary object is to trample a Stetson in the dirt!"

"Young lady, you're in Austin, Texas," Shorty said, joining the conversation. "In these parts ropers and riders are as rampant as fire ants and most of 'em are every bit as poor. When those rangy cowpokes find out you're the daughter of the Hearth and Home legacy, they will be after you like bored bulls to a new salt lick." He cackled at his own humor.

Abby's parents sat side by side beneath an aluminum awning, both wheelchairs locked in the safety position, their hands clasped across the few inches that separated them. She watched and listened with distracted interest while she polished off the plate of sliced beef brisket, creamy coleslaw and tangy mustard potato salad that Guy had graciously prepared. He'd been such a sport, shaking off her prank with a shiver and a laugh.

She scanned the area, teeming with activity and lively conversation, wondering where Guy had disappeared to. He'd delivered her lunch and excused himself.

"Now, go attend to your employees and

their families like the good hostess I'm certain your mother raised. Trust me when I tell you those cowboys will make their own entertainment, they always do," Sarah said, continuing to give orders disguised as advice.

"I may have to find out for myself what sort of entertainment those handsome daredevils make, if you know what I mean." Casey nudged Shorty's foot with her own, and got the conspiratorial grin she seemed to expect.

Abby watched the interaction between her family members and Casey. Where it might have seemed intrusive only weeks ago, today it was amusing, even welcome. If this was what it felt like to have a sister, having five must be amazing.

"Casey, would you give somebody else the opportunity to spoil Dillon and come with me for a while, please?"

Guy's voice sent a surge of pleasant jitters through Abby. She turned about-face in time to catch him jerk his head in a motion that told his sister to join him, and the serious look in his eyes telegraphed urgency. "I need your help with something we didn't anticipate when we arranged this place as our backup site. Now we have a few unexpected decisions to make about this evening's festivities so I need you for about an hour."

Casey strode immediately to Abby's side and planted a loud smacky kiss on Dillon's cheek before handing him over.

"Not a problem, bro."

"Is there anything I can do?" Abby kept her gaze on Guy as she stroked the silky curls on her son's head, then settled him on his feet to toddle off contentedly.

"As a matter of fact there is, but it'll be later this afternoon. Just have a seat, put your feet up and enjoy some more lemonade. Leah knows we'll be out of pocket for a bit, but she's got everything under control."

"What's wrong, Guy?" Abby's mother pressed for details. "My legs may have atrophied but I assure you my brain hasn't. Tell me what's troubling you. Let me help." As always, before she even heard the problem, Sarah Reagan was certain she had the answer.

Guy's eyes narrowed while he appeared to think it over. He was so kind to give the impression he was taking the offer seriously but no way would he do it. Abby was certain of it.

A smile spread across the charming face of the man she'd come to love desperately. With his right hand he snapped his fingers and then pointed.

"You're on, Mrs. Reagan. Let's go for a ride."

CHAPTER SIXTEEN

AT THREE O'CLOCK, Guy stood atop the flatbed of an H&H delivery truck that had been called into service for the day to haul a portable public address system.

"An interesting coincidence has developed that we think everyone will enjoy. We're going to move the final hours of our Employee Appreciation Day activities over to the Luedecke Arena where some of your hometown heroes are about to practice their bareback riding, steer wrestling, team roping and barrel racing. There will even be a mutton bustin' for our aspiring little buckaroos to join in the fun. So you folks come cheer on the local cowboys and cowgirls!"

Hoots and hollers went up from the crowd over the prospect of an impromptu rodeo, an event that even the most urban of Texans claim as genetically ingrained culture.

From Guy's vantage point, he had a clear

view of Abby. He watched her eyes grow round with a mixture of emotions before she looked across the crowd and up into his face. Knowing it had been years since she'd had the freedom and finances to enjoy her sport made the sad smile that flitted across her very kissable lips easy to decipher. As he watched, the light seemed to dawn in her eyes. She shook her head, bent to pick up Dillon and then turned away.

If she knew he'd cooked up the whole scheme as a gift to her, would she view the opportunity to ride as a personal challenge or just one more stressor in her life? And if she agreed to participate, would it be because he asked her to do it for him or because she truly had an interest in reconnecting with the wild-at-heart cowboys of her youth?

Youth.

Guy suddenly felt like an old-timer compared to some of these kids. They would take chances and create physical dares as much for bragging rights as for the prize money he'd personally agreed to put up as a silent sponsor for the hastily arranged competition.

"Y'all enjoy the games and rides for a spell

longer and then mosey on over to the arena," he drawled as best he could.

During the laughter and enthusiastic applause, Guy turned the mic over to Casey. He climbed down the makeshift steps and strode toward the Reagan clan where Abby's back remained turned. She'd squatted, ostensibly too busy with the business of shoelaces to notice him.

Shorty's dark eyes glinted with mischief; his mouth twitched with the effort to hold back a wide grin. Guy had never seen Shorty look more pleased.

"She's on to you two." He wagged a finger at Guy and Sarah. "Claims she won't do it. I got a silver dollar says she will."

Guy turned to Sarah. "And what do you say, ma'am? Will she do it?"

Sarah had been a huge help, riding to the house with Casey, giving instructions on where to find everything Abby would need if she agreed to mount up and ride. Though the woman hadn't been inside her own house for nearly two months, she'd even agreed to wait in the car so no welcome-home surprises would be spoiled.

"I can't say for sure, but she's her father's daughter. If he says she'll run the pattern, my guess is she will." Sarah squeezed Shorty's hand and turned adoring eyes on her husband, giving him credit for their child's tenacity. A trait Guy was certain had been passed down from mother to daughter.

"Once Abigail pulls on those smelly old boots and that sweat-stained hat and she gets a look at the two mounts you lined up, I don't see how she can resist."

"Wish me luck?" He held up both hands, fingers hopefully crossed.

The edges of Sarah's mouth curved upward and she angled her head slightly. From what Abby had said, that was probably the closest thing to approval her mother ever gave.

"You got it…my boy," Shorty agreed.

My boy?

The address caught Guy by surprise. He looked from Shorty to Sarah and back again as he swallowed down what felt like a teaspoon of flour in his throat. He opened his mouth so speak, to say *thank you,* but words fled. The ability to express gratitude that always came so easily was a lost art for long moments while he tried to think of something memorable to say.

"Well, Walgreens Wrangler, you gonna stand there all day or go get my little girl atop a quarter horse for the first time in more than five years?"

"I CAN'T DO IT." Abby's voice gave no clue as to the reason for her refusal. She yanked the tips of Dillon's shoelaces securely, and he was off on sturdy legs, looking for adventure.

"Why?" Guy pleaded. Not that the money mattered, but he'd invested thousands arranging for this "coincidence" and it sounded like she might balk and prove them all wrong.

"I just can't."

"Are you nervous because you haven't ridden in so long? Are you afraid you might get hurt?"

She gave an adamant shake of her head.

"Are you worried about the horses? Because I went to your Rockin' R friend, Garrett, and asked him to personally arrange a couple of seasoned barrel horses for you to choose between. He remembered you and was glad to do it."

She dipped her chin, hid her eyes behind the palm of her right hand. "Oh, Guy, I wish you hadn't gone to all that trouble. Now I'm obligated."

"Don't feel that way, hon. Won't you just relax and have some fun?"

She held her arms out. "I'm dressed for a picnic, not a rodeo."

"Objection overruled. With your mother's help, Casey went back to the house and got all your gear. Sarah is so excited to see you ride again."

Abby's eyes narrowed; the brown depths sparkled with disbelief.

"My mother approved?"

"Of course. She's onboard with everything. And it goes without saying your daddy is, too."

Abby pressed her lips together, stared hard for several seconds.

"Well, what'll it be, cowgirl? You gonna ride with the big boys or sit on the porch?" He tried for a little Texas levity.

She blinked several times. Exhaled loudly and held her palms aloft in surrender.

He opened his arms, an invitation.

She stepped into them and slid her palms around his waist, pressed her cheek to his chest.

I want to be what Abby needs most of all. Right now I think that may just be a good friend, but I want to be so much more. I want to be her everything.

ABBY LISTENED to the cadence of Guy's heart and bit back what she wanted to say aloud.

I've never ridden without Phillip there to support me. Daddy's health kept him away from the dusty arena most of the time and Mother had no interest. At least I never thought she did. All I had was Phillip. One day maybe I'll have a man who wants to be my everything.

"You don't have to do this, Abby. It was just meant to be something fun, something you'd enjoy. If it's not…" His voice rumbled beneath her ear. He held her in the circle of his arms, his large hands lightly stroking the tense muscles in her back. She knew people must be watching, but she had nothing to lose by hugging the man she loved.

"It will be fun. I'm certain of it." She gave

him a quick squeeze, released him from the kind embrace he'd offered and then fluffed her wilting curls.

"We're burnin' daylight, Mr. Hardy. Let's saddle up!"

"Y'ALL GIVE ANOTHER ROUND of applause for Brittany Gennadopoulos on Beauty. Brittany is our reigning champ with a personal best time of 14.897. Up next is Brittany's baby sister Monica riding Cricket. Monica, come a runnin'!"

The announcer's voice boomed over the speakers in the Luedecke Arena, a place Abby had raced dozens of times during her high-school career. Applause and cheers echoed in the alleyway where she sat astride one of the finest quarter horses in the state of Texas.

It had been ages since she'd made a practice run, much less a timed competitive ride and never on an animal this fine. A horse knew nothing of judges or subjective opinions. This event was all about cooperation between a mount and rider. A run against the clock.

With butterflies crowding her belly, she

stretched her legs, pressed downward on the souls of her beat-up old ropers to stand tall in the stirrups. She leaned from the hips and stroked the neck of Restless, the prize-winning sorrel that Garrett had graciously loaned her.

He had remembered her after all. When they'd shaken hands with Guy looking on, Garrett had held hers too long for comfort and said things most young women would have crash-dieted for a week to hear.

"How could a man forget a little beauty like Abby Reagan? You look just like Goldilocks underneath that Resistol." He'd boldly flicked one springy curl with the back of his index finger. Abby had felt Guy stand taller, lean closer. Garrett had noticed, too, because he'd wisely withdrawn the offending hand and hooked his thumb in the front pocket of his jeans before he'd continued.

"Why, I'd have taken a five-second penalty on my best ride if you'd have looked twice at me back then."

He'd been making most of it up, of course, but it was interesting to see Guy's reaction. He'd squinted in that way that accentuated the character lines around his endearing blue eyes and mimicked a smile. But she could tell from the way his neck had tensed that he'd been clenching his teeth. Her mother had assumed the same facial expression when she'd been forced to attend her daughter's public exhibitions, so Abby knew it well. It was ten percent approval, ten percent veneer, and the other eighty percent was annoyance, plain and simple.

The crowd in the arena cried, "Push! Push! Push!" as the rider broke into the last stretch, spurring her horse hard to bring it home.

Abby shivered with nervous excitement. She was up. Everybody she loved was out there in the grandstand, waiting for her.

Everybody but Phillip.

He'd been her champion in all she'd done for as far back as she could remember. And she'd been the same for him. During the years they'd been best friends and for the few months they'd been husband and wife, she'd given Phillip her all. Today would be her last ride dedicated to her first love. And next weekend when she dedicated the playground, she would allow her mourning to come to an end.

It was a time for beginnings. A time for joy.

Time was what she needed most.

If she only had more of it with Guy, she felt certain he would begin to see how much she loved him. He'd shown her with his kindness that he cared. He'd shown her with his kisses that he was interested. But he was a man committed to his career and his family. Was he capable of changing the course he'd set for his life?

More importantly, was he willing?

Restless snorted, shivered his impatience for the open arena and the three barrels that marked the cloverleaf pattern he would run.

Abby put aside all thoughts of spectators and became the partner Restless demanded. She took the lead, began the ritual of kickin' and kissin' that would whip the sorrel into a frenzy as they entered the chute.

"Folks, please help me bring out a young lady who used to be a regular. This is her first ride in a month of Sundays, so give her some encouragement. Let's welcome Abby Reagan Cramer on Restless. Abby, come a runnin'!"

The adrenaline rush hit her full force as the champion barrel horse proved the reason he came with an asking price of forty thousand dollars. She worked the over-under whip attached to the saddle horn and spurred Restless into the arena where they tripped the timer and started the clock.

They took the first barrel with textbook grace. She sat back, grabbed the saddle horn, made the turn and looked for the second barrel. Restless did his job, charging in the direction his rider looked, responding to the pressure of her spurs, the urgency of the whip. They rounded the second barrel in a cloud of dust, searching for the final barrel, heading for the end of the pattern. The drill was perfect once more, second nature to horse and rider.

Now only the home stretch lay ahead. The arena came alive with cheers.

"Ride hard!"

"Haul out, Abby!"

"Bring it home!"

Abby's breathing was as frantic as her mount's. She was certain her lungs would explode. She leaned forward, pushed hard, whipped Restless to give up all the speed his owner was so proud of. The race to the finish was where the heart of the team came alive. The cowgirl and barrel horse did not disappoint as they crossed the electronic timer.

They'd run a clean pattern! There were no penalties! She looked at the timer. Good enough to keep her in the money if this had been a real competition.

"That was Abby Reagan Cramer on Restless with a mighty fine time of 15.599 seconds. Welcome back, little lady. I believe you wanted to say a few words."

Breathless with exhilaration, she guided Restless to the announcer's box. She reached a shaking hand to accept the microphone, worried now that she'd made a mistake by asking for this moment in the spotlight.

She scanned the lower level of the grandstand for the handicapped seating no more than fifty feet away. Her daddy beamed. Her mother smiled brightly. *Really smiled.* Approval was evident in her eyes. Behind them on bleacher seats, Casey and Guy applauded.

GUY'S PULSE HAD RACED right along with Abby, keeping time with the hammering of hooves on the arena floor. He'd never held his breath so tight, clenched his fists so hard, made such a spectacle of himself by cheering so loud. And beside him Casey acted every bit the fool, loving the winning heart behind Abby's effort as much as he had.

He watched her run the tip of her tongue across her lips, saw her chest expand with a deep breath as she raised the mic.

"I won't take long but I need to say thank you to some folks. To the Hearth and Home family for making this day of *dry* fun possible."

The H&H employees laughed and applauded in agreement.

"To my parents for always finding a way to support me and my dreams even when the way seemed blocked."

She hesitated, sounded as if she might choke. Then continued.

"And finally I'd like to dedicate this ride as I always have. To my first love, the man I will always cherish, the one who never let me down. My best friend of ten years. My Phillip."

Guy's breath caught in his throat. Casey

stretched an arm behind him, laid her hand gently on his back.

Abby reached to hand the microphone back, then seemed to change her mind. "Wait, I forgot somebody very important."

Guy's heart quickened, surged with what she was about to say.

"Garrett Ramsey! Thank you so much for the privilege of riding Restless!"

From the other end of the arena, Garrett's loud "Yip! Yip!" could be heard in response. While the crowd laughed, Abby guided Restless out of the arena to cool him down. Guy stood and moved toward the exit with Casey close behind.

"She only had about thirty seconds, bro." Casey knew him too well, felt the need to excuse Abby's oversight.

"That's just it. No matter what I do, I can't even make that woman's short list, let alone her top spot. I'd like to chalk this one up to comeuppance but I'm afraid it's more complicated than that." And more painful.

"You're crazy about that girl, aren't you?"

"It shows, huh?"

"To me, of course. But in the long run it's

probably just as well. Now you won't have any worries about personal complications down the road when the insurance is settled and the investigation is closed."

The investigation. It would never be closed because it had never officially been opened. He'd gone against the procedure established to protect Hearth and Home after his last mistake. He'd chosen instead to protect the Reagans from the scrutiny of a private investigator and now when his father asked to review the file, Guy would have nothing to reveal but excuses.

To complicate matters, he'd challenged the insurance settlement, demanded the carrier review and reconsider the coverage, even insisted on paying out of his own pocket to ensure the Reagans never received another balance-due bill. While he could probably squash that revelation, was it ethical to keep it quiet from his parents? Didn't they have a right to know the person they assumed would be the next CEO of their company had interfered in a corporate settlement?

All because he'd let his intentions to save somebody go too far. He'd strayed from the plan that had always met his needs. He'd let his emotions overrule his good sense.

And he'd only really learned one thing. He'd found the one his heart loved but he was ten years too late.

"GUY SAID WHAT?" Abby couldn't believe what she was hearing. He'd been in the stands cheering her on an hour before and now he was gone. Completely inaccessible, his sister had said, her voice firm, leaving no room for question.

Casey slammed the door securely and rounded the back of the H&H van. She glanced toward the passengers and lowered her voice.

"He said to tell you he had something important to finish up and that he'd see you next weekend at the dedication before he leaves for Galveston. He asked me to escort your mom back to the hospital and get the rest of you safely home."

"Just like that, he left and turned everything over to you?"

"Yeah, stellar, huh?"

"No, it's not at all." Her voice was petulant, irritated.

Casey stared hard, her blue eyes piercing. She folded her arms.

"Well, here's something that is. I never take anything for granted or at first blush. I probe for more facts until I'm satisfied with the answers. And I've done some digging I'm not too proud of at the moment. But here's what I learned, Abby. For the first time in his adult life my brother has put everything he values at risk. And today I watched his face at the moment he accepted that it was a roll of the dice and he may lose it all.

"Because of you, Abby."

CHAPTER SEVENTEEN

EIGHT DAYS LATER, with only her walker for assistance, and her husband right behind in his new motorized wheelchair, Sarah Reagan made her way up the sturdy wooden ramp and entered her home through a much wider door. A small army of Hearth and Home employees in the family room greeted her with a shout of "Happy Mother's Day!"

"Oh, my!" She raised a trembling hand and pressed it to her cheek.

"Welcome home!" they chorused and waved cheerful greetings.

"I wasn't expecting company." Her voice trembled from the shock of surprise guests. Abby suspected her mother would react negatively to a welcoming committee, but they pleaded to stay if only for a few minutes.

"We all need to get back to our families but we have a few things we'd like to show you," Leah offered. "We gave Mr. Reagan a hand with some small changes that will make your home just a bit more accessible." She pointed toward the kitchen.

The volunteers parted to give the lady of the house an unobstructed path. With her head held high, she worked her way across the floor, stopping in a slash of morning sunlight. She nodded her head in appreciation of the wide granite countertops, lowered wall-mount cabinets and non-skid flooring. Her gaze swept the room as she smiled approval. Abby was thankful they'd kept her mother's color schemes intact and had only made functional changes so the room was still familiar, homey.

"How lovely." She pointed to the new ceiling fan.

"That's the one Abby and I always meant to hang."

"Yes, I remember the day we picked it out. But I was referring to the stained glass on the end of the pull chain."

Abby's chest throbbed with the dull ache that hadn't subsided in a week. Of all the lasting marks Guy had left on their home, his small pieces of artwork were the most eye-catching and engaging. How appropriate that one would be noticed right away.

"Look out the kitchen window, honey. The deck was one of our first projects." The pride in her daddy's voice was unmistakable. Guy could take the credit for putting it there, but he wouldn't.

She swept the yellow gingham curtain aside. "Oh, it's wonderful. I can't wait to serve lunch out there. And those cedar barrel planters will be perfect for a summer herb garden." She turned back to the room full of guests, her eyes brimming with gratitude.

"I don't even know where to begin to thank you all." Her gaze dropped; she leaned heavily on the handles of her walker, searching for adequate words.

"Don't tire yourself, Sarah. There's more to see and these nice folks will be at the playground dedication in a few hours. So come with me. Baby girl, you and Dillon bring up the rear. Will the rest of you please excuse us and see yourselves out?" He winked. "My bride needs some privacy in her new boudoir."

The team of volunteers laughed as they shuffled toward the door and out to their cars.

Abby watched her dad take the lead down the long hallway while her mother, who was already an expert at navigating her new support after weeks of physical therapy, stayed close behind.

As she progressed down the hall, she paused to touch each doorway that had been replaced to more easily accommodate a wheelchair or a walker.

At the entrance to what was now truly a master bedroom, she stopped suddenly as if she'd experienced a sharp pain.

"Mama, are you all right?" Abby took a step closer, prepared to transfer all attention from her child to her mother, wondering how she'd ever manage this day in and day out.

Across the room, her father raised his palm signaling all was well.

"She's fine. Just amazed at the changes thanks to the kindness of others. Aren't you, dear?"

Her mother nodded, said nothing. Truly speechless.

Abby surveyed the redesigned and redecorated room as if seeing it as her mother would for the first time. Soft mauve carpet had replaced throw rugs on slippery old oak planks. A beautiful cherry bedroom suite, with the height of the sleigh bed adjusted for easy access, filled the space formerly occupied by inexpensive, decades-old furnishings. Where a wall of dark paneling had loomed in the small bedroom, leaded-glass French doors now opened onto the expanded master bath. The whirlpool garden tub, oversize tiled shower and matching marble sinks were strategically placed to maximize floor space for handicapped access.

In short, it was a luxurious blessing that had never even been a dream before this moment.

Abby's father had positioned himself next to a chair and ottoman that perfectly accented the plush spread on the bed. He patted the thick cushion of the chair and waited patiently until the love of his life settled into it comfortably.

The piercing eyes that had seen life only from a practical view during forty-eight years of marriage now held a spark of delight. "How did you accomplish this, Pete?" She reached for her husband's hand.

"The insurance company has offered us a very generous settlement in addition to paying one hundred percent of your hospital expenses. Of course, nothing's final yet, because you have to approve what the attorneys have agreed to, but Guy went ahead and let us do all the work at cost. The H&H folks provided all the labor so everything would be finished by today."

She laid her head back against the soft cushions, closed her eyes and smiled.

"This is more than we need, more than we deserve. I'm so thankful for coming home to the husband I cherish, and to the daughter and grandson who make our lives complete."

When she opened her eyes and looked at her daughter, there was something there Abby never thought she'd see.

Respect.

"Abigail, don't worry about what the future holds." She squeezed her husband's hand and leaned close to stare into his eyes as she continued to speak to her daughter. "Very soon you too will find the one your heart loves."

ABBY SAT IN THE BACK ROW of the seats set up in their neighborhood community center for the dedication. The darkness of the room, curtains drawn against the midday light, suited her somber mood. She leaned her forearms on the chair before her and rested her head in her hands. Her eyes were closed as she struggled with what she was about to do today.

I am finally going to lay my Phillip to rest and say goodbye to Guy, too.

"Is the seat next to you taken?" Guy's voice penetrated the quiet moment.

Her soul soured at the sound she hadn't heard in over a week. She raised her head. "If you're still willing to sit beside me, that seat is yours anytime you want it."

He sat, reached out his hand. She slipped hers into it without hesitation. The handsome face she'd grown to love was a mixture of feelings. A perfect reflection of the confusion in her heart. His brows were drawn together in concern and though there was sadness in his eyes there was also a spark of hope. The prospect of moving on to a new phase of his life made him even more appealing. The lips that had kissed her so tenderly were pressed together, as if to hold back words that wanted to be said. His chin was low, not in worry but in sincerity, angling his head close to hers.

"Are you ready for this day?" His voice was an extension of the mixed messages that played across his face.

"Definitely." She nodded, certain of what she must do.

"So many people have invested their time, hard work and wise counsel in our family this week. Today is a day of new beginnings for all of us." She cast her eyes down to their hands folded together, squeezed his for strength and resolved not to cry. Dillon's tears, *real tears* as he'd cried himself to sleep asking for Guy the past few nights had been all she could stand. She had to be brave for her son, for her parents.

For herself.

GUY HAD NEVER KNOWN love until Abby. She was so strong in her weakness. She was the epitome of what a woman could do with a heart that had been broken. There was determination in the tilt of her chin, surrender in the softness of her mouth, acceptance and quiet joy in the lovely brown eyes.

"I want to apologize for not being part of that circle of friends who completed the work at your house this week. I need to show you what was so important that it kept me away from you."

She placed the fingers of her other hand against his lips.

"You don't owe me any explanations or words of apology. I understand firsthand why the women you've dated have always wanted to tie you down. You must not realize how strongly you've impacted the lives of others, especially my family. The changes to the house alone are incredible. For the first time in her life my mother was lost for words and that alone was priceless." She smiled, a look of pure pleasure that he intended to put on her face for the rest of his life if she'd have him. If she could only accept him.

"But, Guy, you made the insurance your personal mission and the outcome of that is nothing short of a miracle. Then you sent Casey to finish things here so I could focus on my kids at school. And now you've made the time to come say goodbye in person. You're the kindest man I've ever known."

He didn't deserve her praise. This was not the time but one day soon, before he took her to Iowa to meet his family, he'd tell her everything. How he'd gone home to see his parents to ask their forgiveness for operating outside of company policy. How they'd stood solidly behind his decision to negotiate the most generous possible settlement for the Reagans. How his father had accepted not only Guy's decision to step down, but his personal recommendation to have Casey take his place on the Heart and Home board. How his parents couldn't wait to meet the woman their only son loved.

"Will you stop being the mom in the middle of everything for a few minutes and let me talk?"

"I'm sorry for carrying on like this. You're probably in a hurry to get on the road." She tried to tug her hand free from his, but he held fast to her hand just as he planned to do with her heart.

"I'm not going anywhere unless you tell me that's what you need." He forced the words out, not wanting to give her the opportunity to exercise that right. "Just bear with me for a minute."

He stood, tugged Abby to her feet and led her to the front row of chairs. "Wait here."

On the far side of the room, he reached for the curtain and prepared to reveal the window behind the thick drape that blocked the Texas heat.

He pulled the short cord; the panels swept back; sunlight hit the stained glass and a rainbow cascaded into the room.

ABBY'S BREATH caught in her throat. The splendor of the work was amazing. The splashes of color matched those she had throughout her house in small doses. Guy's unique style, his artist's fingerprints were evidence of his identity. The simple clear window that had formerly afforded a view of the new playground outside had been replaced by a masterpiece of intricately cut and soldered stained glass as fine as those in any thousand-year-old European cathedral.

She crossed the floor as if drawn to the color. Her trembling fingers made contact with the vision. Flowers of every hue leaped to life and seemed to dance, move with the sunlight. Above their swaying heads, a pair of cupped hands released a butterfly.

"Abby." His voice was soft, tender, almost pleading. "I hope you will accept this as my tribute to Phillip, and my gift to your family. I worked on it around the clock all week, hoping that one day you'd see it as a symbol of new life and new purpose. For you."

She didn't wait for him to invite her into his arms. She boldly stepped forward, slipped her hands around him and pulled him close. She tipped her head back to see into the depths of the blue eyes she loved beyond belief.

"I actually see it quite differently."

"You do?" His gleaming eyes reflected the peace and hope she knew must be shining in her own as they pooled with the emotion she wouldn't deny another moment.

"To me it confirms my transformation. I'm a new woman ready for a new love. I've been longing with all my might for that new love to be you. I adore you, Guy. Whatever you do, wherever you go, I will still love you."

"Oh, Abby." He pressed his forehead to hers. She felt a tear fall from his lashes and mingle with her own. "I'm not going anywhere unless you and Dillon are with me. I thought I had things all figured out, but you taught me that my life was unfinished until I found you. Until you found me."

"What about your family business? What about Galveston?"

"I think I've finally got the last laugh with Casey. While she was complaining about all the extra work I was putting off on her, I was really preparing her to step into my job. It's what she's always wanted and now it's hers. I just hope she doesn't let it blind her to what's most important in life."

"And what would that be, Guy?"

"Having a soul mate to love. Having a purpose and a home."

"For you that's Iowa. Mine is here in Texas with my family. How will we make that work?"

He stepped back and extended his hands for her to follow his downward gaze. The fancy boots were gone, replaced by the scruffiest pair of sneakers she'd ever seen. The kind he would only wear at home. She wanted to laugh out loud and burst into tears of joy at the same time. Instead she stepped back into the arms of her soul mate to wait for his answer.

"If your home is here, then mine is, too." His voice dropped to a tender whisper, choked with longing.

"Please, say you'll marry me, Abby."

Yes was too simple. So she answered him with a kiss that said, *I've finally found the one my heart loves*.

* * * * *

HEARTWARMING INSPIRATIONAL ROMANCE

Contemporary,
inspirational romances
with Christian characters
facing the challenges
of life and love
in today's world.

**AVAILABLE IN REGULAR
AND LARGER-PRINT FORMATS.**

Love Inspired® SUSPENSE

RIVETING INSPIRATIONAL ROMANCE

Watch for our series of edge-
of-your-seat suspense novels.
These contemporary tales
of intrigue and romance
feature Christian characters
facing challenges to their faith...
and their lives!

AVAILABLE IN REGULAR
& LARGER-PRINT FORMATS

Love Inspired.

HISTORICAL

INSPIRATIONAL HISTORICAL ROMANCE

Engaging stories of romance,
adventure and faith,
these novels are set in
various historical periods
from biblical times
to World War II.

NOW AVAILABLE!

For exciting stories that reflect traditional values,
visit:
www.ReaderService.com